# Stories of
# China at War

# Stories of
# China at War

Edited by
*CHI-CHEN WANG*

GREENWOOD PRESS, PUBLISHERS
WESTPORT, CONNECTICUT

Library of Congress Cataloging in Publication Data

Wang, Chi-chen, 1899-      ed.
    Stories of China at war.

    Reprint of the ed. published by Columbia Univer-
sity Press, New York.
    CONTENTS: Tuan-mu Kung-liang.  Beyond the willow
wall.--Chen Shou-chu.  Three men.--Mao Dun.  Heaven
has eyes. [etc.]
    1.  Short stories, Chinese--Translations into
English.  2.  Short stories, English--Translations
from Chinese.  3.  Sino-Japanese Conflict, 1937-1945
--Fiction  I.  Title.
PZ1.W22St10 [PL2658.E8]      895.1'3'01      75-26630
ISBN 0-8371-8369-3

Reprinted with the permission of Mr. Chi-Chen Wang

Reprinted in 1975 by Greenwood Press,
a division of Williamhouse-Regency Inc.

Library of Congress Catalog Card Number  75-26630

ISBN 0-8371-8369-3

Printed in the United States of America

# Preface

In *Contemporary Chinese Stories* I did not include anything written since 1937, because, as I said in the preface to that volume, there was then no adequate collection of recent material available in this country from which a representative selection could be made. I am glad that during the past few years I have had an opportunity to examine considerably more material and that I am now in a position to offer a group of stories on various aspects of life in wartime China.

I have arranged the stories in chronological order. "Beyond the Willow Wall," the first in the volume, was written in the summer of 1937: "Under the Moonlight," the last story, was written exactly five years later. The remaining stories fall somewhere in between these two dates, though the date of composition is not always given by the writers. The action of the first story takes place, appropriately enough, in Manchuria, where World War II began; the scene of the last story is laid near Chungking, the wartime capital of China.

The reason why I have not included anything later than 1942 can be found in "Under the Moonlight." In this story the war weariness that had taken possession of all classes of people in China is evident not only in the hero but, to me at least, also in the style of the author. The fact is that the first years of the war saw the greatest literary productivity. The invaders had unified China as nothing had before. There was an air of hopefulness in the land which infected the masses and the intellectuals alike. In the early years of the war Chungking hummed with literary activity almost as Peking did during the Literary Revolution twenty years before. There was a general cry for the evaluation of the new literature as there was for an evaluation of the old two decades before. One of the interesting issues raised at the time was whether the writers, in their professed aim of reaching the masses, should follow the dictum of "new wine in new bottles" (which has the disadvantage of being un-familiar or even unrecognizable to the masses) or "new wine in old bottles" (which has the disadvantage of being heavily contami-nated with old feudal ideas). Among those who believed in the latter method was Lao She (Lau Shaw), who used such "old bottles" as the popular ballad (*ku tz'u*) and the dramatic form of the traditional Peking stage. On a whole, however, there was not much change in the technique of China's wartime literature.

But there is a limit to the suffering which man can bear, and during the war the Chinese writers and intellectual workers have suffered more than any other group. Writing in the November, 1944, issue of the *Hsin Chung Hua,* a Mr. Wu T'ieh-sheng gave some telling statistics on the lot of the writers. Before the war the author's fee represented 58.48 per cent of the total publishing cost; in 1943 it was only 22.3 per cent. The purchasing power of a thou-sand words fell from a picul and half of rice (about 200 pounds) to a little over a *sheng,* one hundreth of a picul. In terms of money, his fee rose only about 50 times, while the average worker earned 150 times more. Mr. Wu mentions the fact that the news-papers of the time carried frequent appeals on behalf of sick and undernourished writers. The fate of I-ou in "Under the Moonlight" was typical of that of most writers rather than an exception.

In addition to the trials of the flesh, there was also the terrible paradox of growing misgivings as the prospects of victory became greater. Unity between the major political parties (which had always been more apparent than real) gave way to mutual jealousy and suspicion. They began to jockey for both political and military ad-vantage, each insisting on saving China in its own way or not at all. Small wonder that during the last years of the war the spirit of hope and faith should have given way to a spell of lassitude and despair.

Since the volume covers a period of only five years to the twenty years of *Contemporary Chinese Stories,* the reader should not be surprised to find it smaller. But within limits I have tried to cover as many different types of material as possible. The activities of the soldiers and guerillas, the peasants and workers are taken up in the first nine stories. They were the real heroes of the war and they have captured the imagination of the writers. But they were by no means all unselfish patriots, as "Purge by Fire" shows. Little Fan is, in a broad sense, as much a traitor as Pao Shan-chin in "Portrait of a Traitor" by Lao She. One aspect of the Japanese military mind —their partiality for the innocuous scholars of the old school—is touched upon in "Test of Good Citizenship." In "They Take Heart Again" Lao She tells the story of a group of intellectuals who were able to rise to the national crisis; in "A New Life" Chang T'ien-yi shows the tyranny of old habits in spite of one's good intentions.

Of the authors represented, four are old timers: Mao Dun, Lao She, Chang T'ien-yi, and Kuo Mo-jo. The first three have appeared in *Contemporary Chinese Stories,* while Kuo Mo-jo is included in *Living China,* edited by Edgar Snow. Pien Chih-lin is a newcomer in fiction but he was already known for his poetry before the war.

Very little is known about the younger writers in this volume. Tuan-mu Kung-liang is a native of the eastern part of inner mongolia, probably from the province of Jehol. He apparently stayed on in the northeast after the Japanese invaded Manchuria in 1931 and worked with various guerilla units until about 1936, when he crossed into free China. During the war years he was active in the Writers Federation. Besides a number of short stories he has written a novel on the landlord class in his native region. He appears to have chosen writing as his vocation. Other authors who have published more than occasional stories are Chen Shou-chu and Yao Hsueh-yin, each of whom has a novel to his credit.

I am indebted to the Chinese News Service for making available to me a group of stories selected by Mr. Pan Kung-chan in Chungking. It is only fair to point out, however, that Mr. Pan is responsible for the selection of six stories eventually included. They are: "Three Men," "Heaven Has Eyes," "Chabancheh Makay," "In the Steel Mill," "They Take Heart Again," and "Under the Moonlight." The translations are made by myself unless otherwise noted.

C. C. W.

Columbia University
August, 1946

# Acknowledgments

Permission to use the following material, not translated by the editor himself, is gratefully acknowledged:

The Red Trousers. Translated by Yeh Kung-ch'ao. Reprinted from *Life and Letters Today*, October, 1939, issue.

An Unsuccessful Fight. Translated by Chu Fu-sung. Reprinted from *China at War*, December, 1943, issue. Copyright 1943 by Chinese News Service.

Chabancheh Makay. Translated by Cicio Mar. Reprinted from *Story Magazine*, May-June, 1939, issue. Copyright 1939 by *Story Magazine*, Inc.

Builders of the Burma Road. Translated by Cicio Mar and Donald M. Allen. Reprinted from *Story Magazine*, March-April, 1942, issue. Copyright 1942 by *Story Magazine*, Inc.

In the Steel Mill. Reprinted from *China at War*, November, 1943, issue.

They Take Heart Again. Translated by Richard L. Jen. Reprinted from *T'ien Hsia Monthly*, November, 1938, issue.

Portrait of a Traitor. Translated by Yeh Kung-ch'ao. Reprinted from *T'ien Hsia Monthly*, August-September, 1941, issue.

The following stories translated by the editor himself have appeared in print as noted:

Heaven Has Eyes. Reprinted from *Mademoiselle*, March, 1945, issue.

Under the Moonlight. Reprinted from *The China Magazine* (formerly *China at War*), June, 1946, issue.

House Hunting. Reprinted from *The China Magazine*, July-August, 1946, issue.

# Contents

# Beyond the Willow Wall[1]

## By Tuan-mu Kung-liang

The ancient Willow Wall stretched across the horizon like an indolent snake; its dark brown back rose and fell with the rolling landscape. Beyond to the north the Heilungkiang spoke in a perpetual whisper, urging the advantages of the land. For here, it says, are mountains capped with snow the year round, here the bears wander about at home and the ginseng grows under the sacred fungus, here gold can be panned from the sands, here almost anything will grow and bear big red spikes of kaoliang if you take the trouble to stick it in the rich, black soil of the plains.

Disguised as dull-looking peasants, Ma Chien and Shih Tou were tramping along the dusty road flanked by fields of tall kaoliang. Shih Tou was preoccupied with his mission. He had volunteered for the firearms extension corps and he was determined to do his best to win one of those coveted ribbons awarded to those who returned with the most guns. Did not Erh Hu-tzu get one? And how proud he was of it! He always made certain that it was displayed to the best advantage and, as if this was not enough, he was forever looking down at it himself so as to draw others' attention to it.

Ma Chien, however, was alert and on the watch for anything that might happen. He was constantly looking around him and listening for unaccustomed sounds above the rustling kaoliang leaves, while he wiped off the sweat that ran down his face and collected around his beard. He was carrying a large, red box of the kind in which cakes are generally packed and had just taken

[1] A long stockade built by the early Manchus to guard against the incursions of the Mongols into Manchuria.

off his belt with the idea of tying it around the box so that he could carry it slung over his shoulder.

"Let's take 'em out, Uncle Ma," Shih Tou said. "I smell something."

"No, there isn't anything. Don't get nervous . . ."

He was interrupted by the sound of gunfire nearby. The two men jumped into the ditch and crouched low. Ma Chien pulled back the false bottom of the cake box, whereupon two Mauser pistols fell out.

"I think it's some crop watchers," Shih Tou said, taking one of the guns.

There was another shot just as Ma Chien was about to say something. This enabled him to identify the type of gun more accurately.

"It sounds like an Iron Cock, don't you think?" he said to his comrade. "My guess is that it's some hold-up man."

"Let's take care of him," Shih Tou said, starting off in the direction of the gunfire, but Ma Chien pulled him back, saying, "Let's mind our own business. We have a job to do."

He proceeded to pack the Mausers back into the false bottom of the box.

"I think we can leave them out until we get near the station," Shih Tou protested. He was one of those who is never happy without a gun. With a gun in his hand he was ready to venture into hell itself, but without it he felt more helpless than a cripple without his crutches.

"Don't be like that," Ma Chien admonished. "If you must hold something in your hand, why don't you break off a kaoliang spike for yourself? What do you think we are out for? You'll only get us into trouble if you don't watch out."

Shih Tou did not pluck himself a spike of kaoliang but busied himself with wiping off his sweat.

"I think we ought to capture at least six guns this time," he said presently. "It ought to be easy."

"Keep that to yourself!"

"Easier than blowing off a speck of dust."

"What's got into you?" Ma Chien said impatiently, his beard bristling on end. "Let me tell you again, you must keep things to yourself!"

For a while the two walked in silence through the gentle waves of the sea of kaoliang. The only sound was the incessant chirping of the insects, dominated by the clear resonant notes of the "iron callers" and the "golden bells." But the silence was soon again broken by Shih Tou.

"Uncle Ma, I suppose we'll get ribbons if we capture fifteen guns?"

"Can't you think of something else for a while? We are coming to the station pretty soon and don't you forget to call me diehdieh [papa]. You mustn't be careless and spoil everything."

"We shouldn't have to wait long at the station," Shih Tou soon returned to the subject. "After we get on the train, we'll cut the signal cord the first chance we get. Then it ought to be simple to disarm the guards, collect the guns, and jump off the train. . . ."

"It is not as easy as you think. Do you think that they'll behave like obedient sons and hand over their guns without a struggle?"

"Who cares? What are a few blackcaps?"[2]

"Enough! my good father," Ma Chien said sarcastically. "Please do keep quiet for a moment. There will be time enough for you to show what you can do when we get there. If you keep on jabbering away, we may lose our lives before we get a chance to carry out our mission. Remember that you are to call me diehdieh."

After this Shih Tou kept still, not so much because he was convinced that Ma Chien was right as because he was beginning to feel annoyed at the latter's nagging. It was not that he couldn't help jabbering; he only wanted to share his enthusiasm and aspirations with his companion. But since the latter insisted on pouring cold water on everything he said, he would keep his thoughts to himself. He would show him. He would capture a dozen guns all by himself and four Mausers into the bargain.

[2] Blackcaps, the puppet government police, in distinction from the redcaps, Japanese military police who wear a red band around their caps.

He'd show them all, show them that he was not all talk and that in spite of his inexperience he was just as good as any of them when it came to results.

Then they'd stick up their thumbs in talking about him!

He saw himself with a ribbon pinned on his chest, the center of attention in the camp on Mushroom Hill. He'd be the proudest of the hundred and twenty elite who had been selected by the commander for the important job of capturing guns.

He even fancied that in addition to the many posters celebrating the completion of the defense works of Mushroom Hill they might put up one reading: "Welcome to Comrade Shih Tou, champion gun capturer."

His thoughts were suddenly interrupted by a train whistle. Ma Chien turned to him and said, "Don't forget now to call me diehdieh."

"I won't," Shih Tou answered, a little testily, with an impatient tilt of the head.

Again they walked on in silence.

"Do you think we'll be able to get a dozen guns?" Shih Tou asked in a loud voice just as a man brushed by him in great haste.

"Are you tired of living?" Ma Chien said angrily after the man had gone out of hearing.

The tone of Ma Chien's voice and the presence of people walking by made Shih Tou realize the seriousness of the situation. He must watch himself from now on. To fail because of circumstances beyond his control would be bad enough but excusable, but to fail because he could not control his tongue would be inexcusable. He decided to keep still and do as Ma Chien told him.

Passing a stretch of privet hedge, they came upon a cinder path, which soon led them to the business section of the town.

The pulse of this busy and prosperous town was the railroad whose trains roared through quiet plains like a fiery monster.

Unceasingly this monster toils from one end of the year to the other. Through summer heat and the bitter winter storms it struggles on with iron resolution, carrying with it tons upon tons of soy beans and kaoliang and corn, lumber and fur, rare medicines such as ginseng and deer's horns, glistening coal and dazzling gold dust. Age seems to have no effect on this monster. On the contrary, the years seem to bring it only renewed vigor and greater capacity for toil. And it carries away with it, besides the produce of the land and excavated riches, quantities of youthful blood and sweat and of the disappointments and shattered dreams of the aged.

Toot! toot! it cries complacently.

Then it returns, bringing with it bright-colored candies, dolls and balls made of rubber, bright cotton prints with short lives, rubber-soled shoes and clacking getas, colorful paper lanterns, soaps and tooth powders, Jintan pills, eye washes and other cure-alls, Asahi beer and Korean apples, cigarettes, and, of course, morphin and heroin, and Friendship, Co-operation, and Co-prosperity.[3]

The lives of those who live near the station are entirely dominated by the railroad. They gear their thoughts and activities to it without ever thinking of revolt.

The man at the crossing always comes out with his red flag at the right moment, the switch man is always at his station manipulating the signals, the despatcher is always on hand at the appointed time and place to deliver the train orders. By long experience the peddlers know on what trains to expect their most generous customers. The livelihood of the porters, ricksha men, and drivers all depend upon the railroad. Hotel agents are there with their flamboyant handbills, which they thrust upon the travelers. They are as inescapable as hungry flies.

Ma Chien and Shih Tou soon came to the square near the station. Shih Tou had a feeling that there were more redcaps and blackcaps than usual and that they all had their eyes fastened on him. He straightened his back and tried to assume as innocent an air as possible.

The square is one of the busiest sections of the town. In the center there is a circular flower bed, with pansies of various colors forming the character for "king"—symbol of the much advertised "kingly way."

[3] Japan's official explanation of the purpose of its invasion.

For the convenience of their patrons the brothel keepers have chosen this strategic spot for their establishments. For here everyone must pass in order to reach his destination and must thus lay himself open to the wiles of the prostitutes parading themselves on the second-story balconies. Indeed there is hardly any one who does not avail himself of the opportunity to cast a passing glance in that direction; some even throw kisses at the ladies as they have seen it done in the movies.

There was, however, one discordant note in this picture. It was that at each intersection there was a police booth, an equilateral triangular structure with windows on all sides. In winter the glass panes are treated with some kind of preparation so that they will not fog or freeze. Thus winter and summer, day and night, the blackcap stationed in the booth was able to watch everything that went on around him and to subject each passer-by to a close scrutiny. He was the symbol of the vigilance and the terror of the New Order.

Shih Tou had walked on without paying much attention to these booths, but the boring eyes of the sinister black spiders, sitting in the center of the net that they had woven, finally unnerved him. It seemed as if they all had their eyes fixed on him, as if they had read his secret. He wished he had his Mauser out instead of in the cake box.

"The sun is very hot," he said to Ma Chien in code. "It makes me sweat."

On his part Ma Chien assumed the air of a knowing father and said, "Don't you keep looking at the bautze shop. It won't do you any good since we can't afford any."

"Dieh-dieh, the bautze is steaming hot," Shih Tou continued, thinking that Ma Chien might not have noticed the policeman and determined to put him on his guard.

"We can't afford it," Ma Chien repeated.

Shih Tou was not sure whether his friend meant by this that there was nothing to fear or that there was no helping it.

Suddenly the blackcap darted out of his booth and headed straight in the direction of Shih Tou.

"Ai-yao-o!" a pitiful cry rose at his side.

Like a timid peasant intent on minding his own business, Ma Chien gave the incident but a passing glance. Then he whispered to Shih Tou, "It's a pickpocket that he is after. Let's be on our way."

Shih Tou would not believe it, and did not stir until he saw the policeman pin his sword on the hapless pickpocket.

They went into the station and bought two tickets. As they approached the entrance to the platform Shih Tou put on the most convincing performance of a worried peasant boy that he could.

"Dieh," he said to Ma Chien. "We've forgotten to take along grandma's tobacco pouch—and the two pairs of wooden soles."

"Ai," Ma Chien grunted approval. He handed the tickets to the checker with slightly trembling hands.

There were redcaps and blackcaps all over the place.

"What is this?" some one asked, pointing to the box Ma Chien was carrying.

"It's cake," Ma Chien said, pointing to his mouth to indicate that it was something edible. To convince the blackcap that the box contained only what it was supposed to, Ma Chien made a motion of offering it to him.

"Would your honor have some?" he said good-naturedly.

"Get out! *Baka desu!*" the blackcap cursed, affecting the idiom of his masters.

Thus Ma Chien got safely through and walked toward the train. When they questioned Shih Tou, all he had to do was to indicate that he was the son of the man just in front.

The train roared on. The trees fell backwards row upon row.

The passengers were a ragged and weary lot, their clothes grease stained and covered with patches. Some dozed with bowed heads, others fixed their eyes vacantly on the passing landscape. Puffs of steam from the locomotive lingered in the air in clouds, hiding momentarily the distant hamlets. Because of the frequent raids on the trains, the planting of kaoliang had been prohibited along the right of way, and the soy and millet both showed the effect of soil exhaustion.

A licensed peddler with a red armband walked through the train carrying a basket filled with sweetmeats and fruits. A squalid-looking child followed the basket with greedy eyes, and the mother, by way of showing her pride, gave it a resounding slap. The child did not cry, for it was resigned to not getting what it wanted, but turned away its head, as if realizing that it had no business to hanker after such luxuries.

"Tickets! Tickets!"

There was a general stir as the passengers got their tickets ready. The collector was closely followed by two blackcaps carrying rifles. Two more blackcaps came in through the door, and then still another, all armed.

There was no sound in the car except the occasional warning of the ticket collector and the click of his punch.

Suddenly a shot rang out. Ma Chien and Shih Tou now each stood upon a seat at either end of the car, their Mausers pointed at the blackcaps.

"Don't be afraid, uncles and brothers," Ma Chien said in a clear voice. "We have come to borrow the guns of these dogs. We are not going to harm anyone else. We are fighting for all of us. We use their clubs to break their legs. No one must move!"

Then he gave orders to the blackcaps, his pistol pointed at them all the while.

"Put your gun down in front of that woman there. Stand up! Now sit down and don't move. Now you do the same thing. Sit down now by that old man and don't move!"

When it came to the last one, he put down his gun as the others had done, but when ordered to stand up, he jumped up and reached for the signal cord.

But the cord had been cut and the man fell of his own weight. Ma Chien despatched him with one shot.

Ma Chien then collected all the guns and strung them on one arm. He retreated backwards to the door, fired one more shot in the air, opened the door and backed out. He tied the guns together with his belt, threw them into the grass, then jumped off the train himself.

At the same time Shih Tou also backed out from his end of the car. As he turned, the door of the next car opened and a blackcap came through. Shih Tou fired and the man fell. Shih Tou jumped across the coupling, stripped the man of his gun and leaped off the train.

The train roared on as if nothing had happened. As it crossed a bridge, it roared out a new burst of vigor.

The crushed grass stained Shih Tou's clothes, but he paid no attention to that. He rushed back to look for Ma Chien. The latter had already collected the guns he had captured, so together they looked for the sixth gun and finally found it in a patch of buckwheat.

The two men looked at each other approvingly and began to think of how to get the guns back to Mushroom Hill.

"First we must carry them under the bridge," Ma Chien directed. "We'll steal some railway ties and make a raft and float down stream to Wukungtun. There will be men waiting for us there."

Shih Tou suddenly felt dissatisfied with the result of the expedition. If the six guns had been all his own work, he would certainly get a ribbon. But now he had to divide the spoils with Ma Chien. It was true that he got one gun all by himself, but that was an accident and he could not possibly claim sole credit for it. But what's the use of only three guns? Maybe Erh Hu-tzu got as many as a dozen all by himself, and would be showing off a bright medal in addition to his ribbon.

"There may be Japanese soldiers under the bridge," he said irritably.

"There aren't any," Ma Chien said. "I know these parts better than you do."

"*Fangpi!* How many times have you been here?"

Ma Chien was surprised at Shih Tou's language, but did not return the oath.

"There must be some one in the hut over there," he said. "I'll go and see what's what. You look after the guns."

He laid the guns in the ditch and walked in the direction of the bridge. Shih Tou flattened himself on the ground and as Ma Chien disappeared from view, the thought flashed through his mind that if a redcap should get Ma Chien, then he, Shih Tou, would be able to lay claim to all the six guns. But the next moment he was red with shame for having thought of such a thing. Surely he had not volunteered for the mission just to show off a piece of ribbon or even a medal! How could he have forgotten the oath of the volunteers!

Presently Ma Chien reappeared, but not alone. There was with him a man thirty-odd years old, of a muscular build. His clothes were covered with an oily grime. Ma Chien introduced him as a man from Shantung, a railroad worker who had decided to join the volunteers. Shih Tou was antagonistic toward him and made fun of him while they fastened the ties together for the raft.

At Wukungtun they learned from the lookouts that all those who went out on gun-capturing missions had returned except Erh Hu-tzu.

That night, back in the stockade on Mushroom Hill, the list of guns captured was posted. Shih Tou was among the first at the bulletin board. It included only names of those who had captured five or more guns. There were twenty-six of them and all were to receive ribbons.

Since Shih Tou had only three to his credit, his name was naturally not there. However, as he glanced through the list, he spotted Ma Chien's name, with "five guns" under it.

There must be a mistake somewhere, Shih Tou said to himself. He knew very well that Ma Chien got only three guns just as he did himself.

He turned away and began looking for Ma Chien. Finally he caught up with him, seized him by the shoulder and said, "Ma Chien, how come that your name is on the list?"

Ma Chien smiled mysteriously and did not reply.

"Tell me, did you turn in a false report?"

"No."

"Then it must be a mistake. You must go and have it corrected."

"There is no mistake," Ma Chien replied calmly.

"Come now," Shih Tou said threateningly, shaking his fist close to Ma Chien's nose. "Tell me what all this means."

"The Shantung fellow has two guns."

"What? I didn't see any guns on him."

"But he has two guns just the same," Ma Chien said.

"What do you mean? Tell me!"

"He has them buried in a tomb," Ma Chien explained. "I didn't want to tell you because I knew you'd let it out and spoil things."

"So that's it," Shih Tou said, and then without warning gave Ma Chien a slap in the face and ran.

For a long time he wandered about the camp in the darkness. Presently he came to a cliff and sat down on a rock. Soon he began to regret his action, realizing that soon it would be known all over the camp and that the men would blame him.

On his way back he was challenged by a sentry. He had wandered off the grounds without first ascertaining the password. He was taken to the commander.

"So it's you, Shih Tou," the commander said with an indulgent smile. "I hear you have struck another comrade."

"Yes, sir," Shih Tou answered and said to himself that Ma Chien must have reported him.

"You must control your temper," the commander said, his husky face assuming a serious expression. "No one has reported you. You may go now!" Then he added, as a patient father would to a son, "And how could you be so careless as to run all over the place without getting the password first?"

Shih Tou did not attempt to explain his grievances and frustrations. However, he could not suppress one question that persisted in his mind.

"Has Erh Hu-tzu come back?"

The commander was silent for a moment and then turning away his face, he said, "He was killed."

Shih Tou staggered out of the commander's room without saying another word, his heart overwhelmed with shame and self-reproach.

Outside, in the direction of the open-air platform, men who were not on duty were assembled under the torch lights. The captured guns were neatly laid out in front of the platform. As the bonfire rose, two men carrying a stretcher slowly approached the assemblage. On the stretcher lay the body of Erh Hu-tzu wrapped in white.

*Summer, 1937*

# Three Men

## By Chen Shou-chu

With baskets on their backs, Hsiao Hei-tzu and Mao San-lang
emerged from the village and walked on in silence one behind
the other. It was May and the rice paddies were just a few inches
above the flooded fields. It was the time of the year when the frogs
had wearied of their croaking and the "get-you-busy" birds had
flown from the countryside but when the cicadas had not yet
climbed up to their perches in the trees and the "lady-weavers"
were still waiting in the earth for the pumpkins to flower. May
is ordinarily a busy month for the farmers, but this year there
was a conspicuous lack of activity everywhere. An oppressive
silence had descended on the countryside like a dark cloud. People
on the road were not given to talk, and the workers in the fields
went about their tasks without benefit of their folk songs. Even
the irrigation wheels seemed to turn more slowly than usual and
to emit a mournful sound.

Hsiao Hei-tzu felt the necessity of doing something to relieve
the pent-up, oppressive feeling that weighed heavily on him, but
he did not feel like talking to Mao San-lang, though the latter
was like a brother to him. He tried to sing but his voice cracked
in the second line. He spat in disgust and sang no more. Mao
San-lang paid no attention to him but walked on in silence behind him.

Presently they saw a middle-aged man walking toward them in
an unsteady gait. As he drew nearer they saw that he was mum-
bling to himself and occasionally stamping his foot to emphasize
his grievance.

"Here comes Tsui Pa-hsien," Hsiao Hei-tzu said, and ran forward, followed by Mao San-lang. It was indeed Tsui Pa-hsien, the village drunk. His shirt was partly torn in front, exposing his breast, and there were scratches on his face. He stood still as the two younger men ran up to him.

"What has happened, Uncle Pa-hsien?" Hsiao Hei-tzu asked.

"Did you run afoul of *them?*" Mao San-lang suggested.

"No," Tsui Pa-hsien said with a contemptuous air. "It is not time to settle accounts with those sons of turtles yet. I am no fool. Why should I buck them now? But we'll settle with them one of these days, make no mistake about it."

"Then what was it?" Hsiao Hei-tzu asked, no longer so interested as before.

"Just another drunken brawl, then?" Mao San-lang suggested with a sneer. '

"You are right," Tsui Pa-hsien admitted sheepishly. "I suppose it is all my fault. I just can't leave the yellow liquid alone, weakling that I am!" So saying, he slapped his own face, much to the amusement of Hsiao Hei-tzu and Mao San-lang. Then he continued, "It's true. When those sons of turtles came to town I swore to Heaven that I'd sooner die than go there to guzzle that yellow liquid. Of course I love the stuff. I have been drinking if for more than twenty years and from the way I feel I won't be here to enjoy it ten years from now at the most. I swore off not because I want to give up drinking but because I do not want to have to go to the next town and let those sons of turtles, those bandits, soil my sight. I may be a drunk but I am pretty particular about the people that I mix with. But really, we are a useless lot nowadays. If we had now a Kuan Kung or even a Chao Tzu-lung or a Wu Sung, those sons of turtles would not have such an easy time of it. They'd long ago have been kicked out of here and back to where they belong. Now with only about twenty of them in the town, they have the surrounding countryside completely cowed. They are treated as if they were gods, heavenly deities on earth. Now, tell me . . ."

"Enough, Uncle Pa-hsien," Hsiao Hei-tzu said with a sly smile. "We are pretty good when it comes to talking, but when we meet one of them we don't dare not bow and scrape, or even kowtow to them."

"I have never had to do that," Tsui Pa-hsien said, beating his chest, and then added knowingly, "I have a secret, you see. I'll tell it to you: when you go to town, you must take your eyes along with you. If you see the Japs to the east, then you walk west. If they are in the west, then you walk east. In other words, never meet them face to face."

"Uncle Pa-hsien, whom did you get into a fight with?" Mao San-lang asked.

"It makes me mad just to think of it," Tsui Pa-hsien said. "It was with Wang Lao-pan. I can hardly believe it myself. For I am old customer of his; I could have bought myself a piece of land and got myself a wife with all the money I spent on liquor at his place. If it had not been for my weakness for that yellow stuff I could have a family by now, maybe with a son older than you. As for him, he probably would have had to close up the place if it had not been for my business. Well, it had been more than ten days since I went into town. Naturally I went straight to his place. I ordered eight coppers' worth of wine and two coppers' worth of salted beans. I could not believe myself but I swear I got only three drinks out of the pot. So I ordered another eight coppers' worth but this time I looked into the pot and sure enough I found there's only four copper's worth in it. So I said, 'You have made a mistake here, Wang Lao-pan. The pot is only half full.' 'I didn't make any mistake,' he said, 'but the price of liquor has gone up.' That made me mad. That's the trouble with tradespeople. So I said he could not raise the price on me and moreover it's only ten days since I was last there. Then he bent over me and told me a long hard-luck story about the shops that had been robbed and the new taxes that have been imposed. I have heard about a lot of taxes in my time but never the fancy ones which Wang Lao-pan mentioned. Moreover, he said he knew where all money went, pointing stealthily in the direction of Wu Ta-yeh's house, where as you know, the Jap turtles are staying. That was not the worst of it either, he said, for they would come and drink quantities of liquor and refuse to pay. And you can't close up, he said, because they'd charge you with trying to create a panic. I got tired of listening to him, so I gave him a push like this"—here Tsui Pa-hsien gave a demonstration of how he did it that almost sent the unwary Hsiao Hei-tzu sprawling on the ground—"and said that what they did was no concern of mine and that he just could not raise the price on me. I must say that Wang Lao-pan is pretty deecnt sort, for he poured me a cup on the house. But I was still pretty mad and decided that I would not come again to drink but that I might as well drink to my heart's content while I was at it. So I ordered another eight coppers' worth."

"Uncle Pa-hsien," Hsiao Hei-tzu said, "you haven't told us about the fight yet."

"Don't hurry me. That came after I drank the last eight coppers' worth I ordered. To tell the truth, I was really thinking of the Jap turtles while I was hitting Wang Lao-pan, and I suppose it was the same with him, since they were responsible for his losing money. Anyway, after I finished drinking the wine I wiped my mouth and said that I was sorry but that he'd have to mark it down. But he said I couldn't do that because times were different. So I told him that he was a dog to oblige the Japs but not an old customer. That made him mad and he said that I shouldn't pick on him. I said he was picking on me and not me on him. So I held out my fist and he held out his . . ."

"I don't think Wang Lao-pan was at fault," Mao San-lang said.

"It wasn't my fault either," Tsui Pa-hsien said, beating his chest.

"It was neither your fault nor his," Hsiao Hei-tzu said. "It's all because the Japs have come to town."

"That's right, it's all because the Japs have come to town," Tsui Pa-hsien agreed as he staggered away in the direction of the village.

About a mile from the village there is a lake known as the White Goose Bay, the scene of the dragon boat race in former years. The Dragon Boat Festival belonged primarily to the young men of the villages, for it gave them a chance to show their skill at boxing and sword dancing on the gayly decorated boats and to win honor for their particular village. Hsiao Hei-tzu and Mao San-lang had represented their village the two previous years and had won wild applause from the spectators. Now they stopped at the scene of their former triumphs and surveyed the wide expanse of water with a sense of regret.

"If we had followed Tien Lao-ta's suggestion, the lake would be a busy place by now," Hsiao Hei-tzu said.

"You can't blame people for not wanting to hold the boat race in a time like this," his companion said. "What a time to live in, never knowing what's going to happen next." He was silent for a moment and then said, "I would not take part even if they had decided to hold the race as usual."

Hsiao Hei-tzu looked at his friend uncomprehendingly at first but then said knowingly, "I see why now."

"Why, then?"

"Because there is no one to applaud and give you inspiration."

"I don't know what you are talking about."

"Don't pretend. You have not been the same since she died. You have no mind for anything."

Mao San-lang was silent, his head bowed.

"There is no use in hankering for the flesh of the swan. She is not your morsel even if she weren't dead."

"Nor is she yours," Mao San-lang retorted.

"But I never had any such aspirations."

"Neither had I! But you! you were fit to hang when the Japs made off with her."

"Let's not pretend that she didn't mean anything to either of us," Hsiao Hei-tzu said seriously. "She was very decent to both of us. Just think what a terrible way it was to die, with more than ten Japs . . ."

"The sons of turtles! the bandits!" Mao San-lang swore.

The two friends now quite forgot their old jealousies. They began to talk freely about the girl whom they had both admired and to exchange confidences. They both swore that they would avenge her death.

White Goose Bay was flanked on one side by a pine-covered

hill known as Little Ox. It was not much of a hill but it was steep enough to discourage agriculture and was little frequented except by cowherds and grass cutters.

Hsiao Hei-tzu and Mao San-lang had come out to gather grass but by the time they reached pine forest they were too occupied with their thoughts to set to work in earnest.

"Let us really kill a few Japs instead of just thinking about it!" Mao San-lang suddenly said.

"I am thinking of the same thing," Hsiao Hei-tzu nodded in agreement.

"Let's take a solemn oath," Mao San-lang said.

"Let's do," the other man agreed, whereupon they both knelt down toward the sun and uttered the formula that they had heard on the stage. But they were interrupted by the sound of a horn. They looked down on the road and saw a man coming in their direction on a bicycle.

"A Jap!" Hsiao Hei-tzu cried.

"Down!" Mao San-lang warned. Both flattened themselves in the grass and held their breath. The bicycle drew near and in another moment had whirled by them. They both got up and looked at each other without saying a word. For a while they pretended to cut grass but they soon gave it up.

"He was alone," Hsiao Hei-tzu said, "and he was unarmed. We could have fixed him if we weren't so scared."

"That's right," Mao San-lang said regretfully. "We musn't miss the opportunity the next time.

"But you won't often find them alone and unarmed."

"If we only had guns ourselves! We could hide in the grass or in a cave and pick them off as they came."

"That gives me an idea," Hsiao Hei-tzu said. "Come with me."

Farther up the hillside there was a cave about half the height of a man. Standing inside one could look down on the road about thirty feet away. Hsiao Hei-tzu took Mao San-lang up there, jumped into the cave, picked up a rock and hurled it down at the road.

"This is what we can do."

Mao San-lang followed his example and said, "I think it will work all right."

"Let us practice a little first," Hsiao Hei-tzu said. "Supposing you go down on the road and pretend that you are a Jap and let my try to hit you."

"But be careful not to hurt me," Mao San-lang cautioned as he walked down the slope.

"Of course. I'll just use a pebble no bigger than a bean."

Mao San-lang thrust out his chest and started goose-stepping down the road. Hsiao Hei-tzu laughed and said, "You don't have to do that. You are not on the drill ground. Just walk naturally."

Mao San-lang tried again but this time he stopped when he got near the cave.

"What's the idea of stopping?"

"So that it will be easier for you to hit me."

"Don't be silly. Do you think a Jap would stand still for you to hit him?"

Again Mao San-lang walked back and started in the direction of the cave. The pebble hit him squarely on the back.

"Let me try again," Hsiao Hei-tzu shouted with glee. "Come running this time."

Mao San-lang obeyed and Hsiao Hei-tzu hit him again, this time on the chest.

"Just once more," Hsiao Hei-tzu said. "Go farther back, beyond the bend, and run as fast as you can when you come within range. After this I'll let you throw it."

Mao San-lang followed the instructions. Presently he appeared around the bend but instead of running down the road he scampered up the hillside.

"What are you doing?" Hsiao Hei-tzu shouted at him.

Mao San-lang motioned him to keep quiet. He got into the cave and whispered, "Here comes one!"

"Did you see him?"

"No, but I heard him sing and I know it's a Jap because I couldn't understand a word of it."

"Quick, let us get some rocks and wait in the cave. They can't see us from the road. If there's only one of them, we'll attack him. If there are more of them, we'll just keep quiet."

The sound of singing drew nearer and soon a Japanese soldier appeared around the bend. He was alone but armed. He stopped abruptly in the midst of his song as a rock about a size of a fist struck near him. As he unstrapped his gun for action, a second and a third piece of rock flew at him. One of these hit him on the leg. As he fired an even larger missile hit him on the chest and felled him. The two men jumped out of the cave and rushed upon him. Hsiao Hei-tzu grabbed for his gun while Mao San-lang knelt on him to hold him down. The Jap pulled out his bayonet but Hsiao Hei-tzu caught his wrist and after a brief struggle turned the weapon against the foe's throat and cut it.

For a while the two men stood over their victim, paralyzed, but they soon recovered, and after a brief consultation decided to throw the body into the lake. They tied a heavy rock to it and stopped the flow of blood with some earth. They stripped the cartridge belt off the body and hid it in the grass with the gun. Then they carried the body to the lake and threw it in. After making sure that the body was not going to float up they returned to the motor road and scraped off the blood stains. Then they went into the forest and sat on the grass around their booty, still incredulous of what they had just done.

"I never thought that it would be so easy," Mao San-lang said. "No more difficult than squashing a flea."

"They are pretty useless in a fair fight," Hsiao Hei-tzu said. "After all they are so small, hardly bigger than children. What can they do without their weapons?"

"This is very much like what the merchants' militia men used to carry," the other commented as he examined the rifle. "We don't have to use stones the next time. Let's try it out." He stood up and fired into the air. The report reverberated in the air and Mao San-lang shook with excitement.

"This will be a great help," Hsiao Hei-tzu jumped up and took the gun. He was about to fire another shot but thought better of it. He turned on the safety catch, saying, "We had better save ammunition. We must find a place to hide it. We can't take it back to the village."

They found a crack in the stone not far from the cave, laid their booty in it and covered it up with grass and pebbles. They had forgotten all about the grass and it did not occur to them that they might arouse suspicion if they went home empty-handed until they were half way there. They stopped along the road and cut some. They were excited and confused. One moment they would be afraid that their deed had been discovered already and that the Japs would come to wreak revenge that very night. In another moment they wished that they could tell the whole village about it so that they would be welcomed as heroes. But caution prevailed and they went quietly home.

Nothing happened that night. Early the next morning Hsiao Hei-tzu went to the pine forest to make sure that their secret had not been discovered. There he found Mao San-lang bent over their cache.

"We must get another, so that we'll each have a gun," Hsiao Hei-tzu said.

"I am thinking of the same thing," Mao San-lang said. "Let us wait here. Maybe another one will come along."

"I am afraid it won't be any use waiting today," Hsiao Hei-tzu said. "The dwarfs are a pretty clever lot. They won't be coming this way just after they have lost one of their men."

Not long after their return to the village, one of the villagers who had gone to town early came back and told the news. The Japs had discovered that one of their number was missing and were arresting people right and left. Among them was Wang Lao-pan the tavern keeper. Moreover, they were going to make a search of the surrounding villages.

The atmosphere of the village became tense at the news and there was considerable difference of opinion regarding the deed. Some expressed admiration for the unknown hero but others said that it was senseless and foolish and that it would only bring retaliation against people in the surrounding countryside as a whole. Some thought that the Japs might have made up the whole story as an excuse for more extortion.

That day everyone stayed away from the fields, for fear that the Japs might come down to make arrests. Not that it made any difference where they hid: the Japanese could search them out in their houses too. But generations of community life have instilled in the village people a strong feeling for their group. They feel more secure as a group and are quite helpless when caught away from it.

The town was not far from the village, but because no one dared to venture forth the village became completely cut off. When Tsui Pa-hsien did not come back by dusk, the villagers feared the worst. They did not go to bed after supper as they usually did but got ready to flee at a moment's notice. The women packed bundles of clothing, the men got ready their baskets and poles for carrying their heavier household utensils and children too young to walk. They were ready to vacate their homes at the first signs of the approaching Japanese.

However, the night passed without incident. The next day Tsui Pa-hsien returned toward evening, haggard and with bruises on his arms and knees. He was not inclined to talk but pressed by the villagers for information he briefly told them what had happened. The day before he was in Wang Lao-pan's place when he heard a commotion in the street. He was grabbed by a Japanese soldier as he tried to get away from the town. Forty-seven had been seized and locked up in Wu Ta-yeh's place. They were questioned one by one but as no evidence was found against them they were released the next day. "It served the Japs right," he concluded. "They have not treated us like human beings and it is only natural that some of us should try to pick them off. Not only do I know nothing about who did it. Even if I did I would not tell."

Hsiao Hei-tzu and Mao San-lang went to call on him after supper, taking with them a pot of wine. They found, contrary to usual custom, a light in his room, but he blew it out when he heard the two men approach. He relit the lamp when he found who his visitors were.

"What are you looking for, Uncle Pa-hsien?" Hsiao Hei-tzu asked.

"I was looking for—oh, nothing in particular," Pa-hsien answered soberly, his eyes fixed on his visitors. Then seeing the bottle Mao San-lang was carrying, he asked, "Is that wine you've got there?"

"Yes," Mao answered. "We heard what the Japanese turtles did to you and so we have brought this to cheer you up."

"How do you know that they have done anything to me?" Pa-hsien asked with some irritation. "I got back all right, didn't I?"

"We knew about the bruises you carry on your arms and legs," Hsiao Heit-zu said solicitously.

"It's so good of you two to think about me. This is the first time in my life . . ."

"It's so stupid, whoever did it!" Hsiao Hei-tzu pretended, watching closely Pa-hsien's reaction. "What's the good of killing one or two of them? It only brings trouble to everyone. Such people . . ."

"But this is exactly the kind of people we need," Pa-hsien protested. "They are brave men, heroes. I don't blame them at all. I only regret that I don't know who they are, for if I did I would go and kowtow to them."

"Have a drink, Uncle Pa-hsien," Mao said, passing him the bottle.

Pa-hsien hesitated for a brief moment before he took the bottle. Then he took a long draught and began to talk defiantly, gesticulating and thumping the table. "Those sons of turtles! I, Lao Pa, have never been one to trifle with. I have never bothered them, yet they picked on me! If I ever have the chance I'll kill them and skin them. You just watch. They kicked me when I would not kneel down, and they beat me to make me confess to something that I know nothing about."

He suddenly stood up, went to the corner of the room and took out an iron rod concealed there. Then turning to the two young men, he asked, "Don't you two fellows often go to the pine forest to cut grass? Do you often see Japanese pass by there?"

The two men were taken aback by the questions. Hsiao Hei-tzu then answered, trying to assume an air of indifference, "We have been told that they often pass by that way, so we have not gone there for some time."

Pa-hsien took up the bottle and drained it dry. "I am an old man now," he said, "and my strength is gone. You are still young and strong of limb. But frankly, it seems that I shall have to play the role of a hero instead of you young ones." He laughed as he concluded.

Hsiao Hei-tzu and Mao San-lang left Pa-hsien with their hearts bulging with delight. To be praised without being known—this is pleasure indeed. They were inspired by this praise and were no longer afraid.

Early the next morning they went directly to their cache and brought forth the gun, ammunition, and bayonet. They did not even make a pretense of cutting grass; they left their baskets home. They concealed themselves in the cave and waited for their chance. But no one appeared on the road. Getting tired of waiting, they sat down, drew a kind of chess board, and amused themselves by playing with pebbles.

Just as they were getting absorbed in their game, they suddenly heard some one call "Halt!" followed by a gun shot. They stood up and looked out on the road. There they saw two Japanese soldiers firing into the wood. The unexpected sight unnerved the two men. They ducked down and for a while did not dare to move. Suddenly Hsiao Hei-tzu gritted his teeth, stood up and fired a shot without aiming. The bullet went wild and flew over the heads of the Japanese soldiers. The latter immediately wheeled around and fired in the direction of the cave. Mao San-lang had been quaking with fright but he recovered sufficiently to pick up the rocks which he had piled up previously and throw them down at the enemy. Hsiao Hei-tzu took more deliberate aim and fired. It hit one of the Japanese in the chest and brought him down. The other stood still for a moment, uncertain as to what to do. He fired a few shots tentatively toward the cave. When no shots were fired in return, he stopped and began to climb up the high ground opposite the cave so that he could command a view of it.

Meanwhile the two men in the cave were paralyzed with fear. They crouched on the floor of the cave and waited for their fate without any thought of further resistance. They did not even dare to look out. But suddenly there was a sharp cry, followed almost immediately by the sound of some metallic object falling on the ground.

"Come on now, I have got him!" a familiar voice called. The two companions looked out just in time to see Pa-hsien pick up his iron rod and hit the fallen Japanese as he struggled to get up.

"Uncle Pa-hsien!" they both shouted and scampered down from their perch.

"So it is you two! I was wondering who could it be that saved my life."

The Japanese again struggled to get up. Mao San-lang felled him with a blow of his fist. Pa-hsien then struck him on the head with his rod and finished him off. After burying the bodies and concealing the guns, the three men sat down and compared notes.

"I made up my mind last night that I would go after them," Pa-hsien said. "So I came here this morning with my iron rod and waited for my chance. I got tired of crouching in the grass and thought I would practice a little with the rod. In the midst of it two Japs appeared out of nowhere and leveled their guns at me. To tell the truth, I was so scared that I almost fell over. I turned and ran. One of them called 'Halt!' but I paid no attention to him. Fortunately there was a boulder near by. I ducked behind it. They fired a shot at me but it didn't hit me. Then I heard a shot from another direction and the Japs walking away. I peeped over the boulder and saw one of them fallen on the ground. I knew I had help but I had no idea that it was you two. I crawled out from behind the boulder and saw the other climbing up the hillside not more than twenty feet from me. I threw my rod at him and luckily I hit him. If it weren't for you two, I would have been killed."

"And if it were not for you, we too would have fallen into the hands of the Japs," Hsiao Hei-tzu said with a sigh.

"We have three guns now, one apiece." Mao San-lang clapped his hands.

"We ought to get five of them next time, the sons of turtles," Pa-hsien said.

"That will mean another five guns," Hsiao Hei-tzu said. "We'll get five men to join us. We shall then kill at least ten of them, the sons of turtles!"

They laughed and jumped up and down in glee.

The sun was then directly over the tree tops, time for the laborers in the fields to return home for their noon meal.

*December, 1938*

# Heaven Has Eyes

## By Mao Dun

Chang Wen-an started up at the bugle call. His eyes were heavy and he could hardly open them, but he knew well that the insistent notes meant a general alert.

Three years in the army had given him a special faculty: he could dress in his sleep. However, he suddenly became awake, though the bugle notes continued to ring in his ears. The papered window was beginning to turn a grayish white. After staring vacantly for a while, he said, laughing a little, to himself, "Pooh, it's only a dream."

He leaned back in bed, his mind passive and without direction. Innumerable and diverse thoughts pressed against his brain, clamoring for admittance. Gradually, out of this confused and clamoring mass one thing raised its head above the others. By this time Chang Wen-ang was completely awake. He regained his power of thought and began to recall his dream.

Half a month ago he had decided, after a period of hesitation, to ask his commander for an indefinite furlough, because of an illness from which he suffered and which the army surgeon was unable to diagnose. His request was duly granted, and he took leave of his division, which he had been with for more than three years, and the X war area, where our lines jutted irregularly into the enemy's. When he had first joined the division, he was a master sergeant; now he was a staff officer with the rank of captain. With his papers he received a traveling allowance of a thousand dollars and another thousand which his commander gave him for medical expenses. On the eve of his departure his comrades had given him a farewell dinner, but just as they were warming up to their wine, the general alert had been sounded. There was nothing unusual about such alerts, but on this occasion his friends commiserated with him and expressed the fear that he might not be able to leave the following day. Then they congratulated him when the alert turned out to be a false alarm. He was greatly moved by their solicitude and he who was not ordinarily given to self-expression said to them: "If the enemy should attack, it wouldn't matter if I did not get away. I should be glad to share for another time our common destiny!"

Now on his first night home, the bugle call that sounded the last alert while he was with his division had invaded his dreams.

Fragments of his dreams began to come back to him, like chickens emerging cautiously from their corners after having scattered at the threat of some danger. They made a confused mass of fear and joy, of bitter and sweet, of the past and the future, of reality and fancy. Now he was living vividly in his dream again. He had managed to buy an ox and had brought it home. The unexpected gift had occasioned the same indescribable look of surprise and joy on his parents' faces as had his unannounced arrival the day before. Then just as his father was patting the ox on the back, his face wreathed in smiles, the general alert had been sounded suddenly. Whereupon the ox of his dreams of the future vanished, its place taken by a flash of reality out of the past.

Chang Wen-an grinned broadly, his heart suffused with a delicious happiness though it had been but a dream. On his journey home he had been trying to figure out how best he could make use of the money which he had securely sewed into his pocket. His commander when he handed Chang Wen-an the money had earnestly bade him not to squander it but to use it for medicine and nourishing food so that he might get back his health. Chang Wen-an had promised that he would take care of himself. But on the very first day of his journey, he began to entertain different ideas.

He had no trouble in persuading himself that there was nothing seriously the matter with him, nothing that a good rest and good food would not cure. He felt that he ought to give the thousand dollars to his parents and let them make some better use of it. What would they do with it, he wondered, and kept on wondering about it on his long journey home. He knew what his mother wanted. There were the repairs to be done to the house, and she had been after him to get married. As for his father, Wen-an knew that he had always hoped to buy another ox ever since they lost their strong, brindled beast in the last civil war, but he had never been able to scrape together enough money for the purpose. The son imagined how his parents would argue over their pet projects and how his father would say: "Wen-an, my son, the money was given to you by your commander for medical expenses. You should not use it for anything else."

As he thus revolved the problem in his mind he would put his hand over his inside pocket to make sure that the bills he had securely sewed up in it were still there. Finally he struck upon a wonderful scheme: he would say nothing about the money to his parents. After resting at home for a day, he would go to the next town where his Uncle Tung lived and buy an ox and bring it home to his parents as a big surprise.

The more he thought about his scheme and contemplated the effect it would produce, the more pleased he became. The vision of a beautiful yellow ox with liquid eyes appeared before him, lying there in placid contentment, chewing its cud with a slow, rhythmic sidewise motion of its lower jaw. He could not help laughing out loud at this beautiful picture. The laugh woke him to reality. Looking up he found the papered window now turned a bright pink. In the next room his parents were up and about, his father coughing, his mother emptying something into a basket.

It had been rather late in the day when Chang Wen-an reached home. His parents, mindful of his need for rest after a long journey, had urged him to retire early. They themselves, however, were too excited to go to bed. They spent the evening visiting their neighbors and breaking the happy news to them. His father even went as far as his favorite tea house more than a li away and there proudly confided his happiness to his cronies. He asked them about the rank of staff captain, how high it was in the military hierachy, for he was already planning to sell a picul of grain and give a feast to celebrate his son's triumphant return, and he had to know his son's station so that he could invite some appropriate guests.

So it was that the news of Chang Wen-an's return was all over the village. And before the sun had dissipated the morning mist, his house was already filled with visitors. They spoke all at once and bombarded him with all sorts of questions, so that he became flustered and did not know whom or what to answer first. He could only answer in the vaguest terms: "Fine, fine, everything is fine at the front. They are putting up a good fight. Rations? Of course, that's fine too. After all, are they not right on the front lines?" However, he felt apologetic for not being able to tell them about things in more concrete terms. He felt their look of disappointment upon him and knew what they were thinking of: we have heard all that before, they seemed to say.

Their gaze embarrassed him. He tugged at the end of his coat and was as nervous and scared as a prisoner at a court martial. After a while he said with some confidence, paraphrasing the familiar words which his superior officers had often used in exhorting the men: "Of course it is not easy at the front. It is often quite hard and bitter. But then are we not fighting the Japanese devils? For the sake of the country, should we not all bear whatever hardships are necessary?" Then he stopped and smiled sheepishly.

Now the conversation became desultory. Chang Wen-an's father and the older visitors talked about old times and new, and marveled at the changes that had taken place. Some of the young visitors pressed around Chang Wen-an and asked him about men in the village who were at the front.

"I don't know," he said after some hesitation, shaking his head, and then, anticipating their dissatisfaction, he hasitily added: "Really I don't know. You have no idea how vast the front is. It stretches for a distance of several thousand li, and is divided into many theatres. Even if we were in the same theatre, we may not be in the same army group, and even if we were in the same army group, there are thousands and thousands of us. If I ran into anyone from the village at all, it would be only by pure accident."

"We didn't think you would know," someone remarked sarcastically.

"Let us ask him just one more question," another said, just as Chang Wen-an was about to defend himself. "If he doesn't know about this man either, then he is truly a lantern with a black lacquered shade. Now this man has been away for over four years and has been to many places. He was at the battle of Chang-sha and has been in the provinces of Hupeh and Kiangsi. He did not join the army empty-handed either but took with him four pack horses and a helper. Do you know anything about him?"

"That's right," chimed in a third. "He hasn't been heard from for more than two years now and his son has been asking about him everywhere."

"What's his name?" Chang Wen-an asked, with the puzzled look of a student confronted with an unexpected question.

"Yes, what's his name?" someone repeated the question sarcastically. "You can trace a person without knowing his name."

"Yes, of course he has a name," another said impatiently; "and it's Chen Hai-ching. He lives on the other side of the hill."

"Oh, Chen Hai-ching!" Chang Wen-an repeated, recalling now that before he himself joined the army Chen Hai-ching had made himself the chief topic of conversation in the neighboring villages by offering his services and his pack horses to the transport corps, leaving behind him an aged mother and a wife and son. He had never met the man, but he remembered the name well, a name that had haunted him until he himself made up his mind to go the front. His eyes brightened as he said, "Chen Hai-ching! Of course I know about him!" Then he stopped abruptly, filled with misgivings, for not only had he not met the man at the front but he had not even had time to think about him since he himself entered the service. However, he could not bear to make himself look any more ignorant than he was in the neighbors' eyes already. So he temporized, "Chen Hai-ching! why, he is all right."

He winced at his own words, for they sounded hollow even to himself. Fortunately, no one noticed his predicament. The man who first asked about Chen Hai-ching said with a sigh: "He may be all right, but his horses are gone. His son got a letter from him year before last, saying that two of them were bombed to bits by the devils' airplanes, another was killed by a shell, while the remaining one got sick and died. You'd think that he would come back after that, but no. He became a combat soldier and vowed that he would not come back until the last devil had been driven from the land. It's good to hear you say that he is all right. It's almost two years now since his family has heard from him."

"So—" Chang Wen-an began, but when he noticed the eager eyes around him, he decided to keep his ignorance to himself and said instead: "So he hasn't been heard from for more than two years. But he's all right. Chen Hai-ching is a brave man, a man of iron, and a man like that never gets killed. He is a good man, too, and bullets do have eyes and will not strike a good man." He became quite excited by his own words, though he was not sure whether they were true or merely represented how he believed things should be. "I think he ought to be a private first class now, or even a corporal or sergeant. Yes, Chen Hai-ching—he is a credit to our district."

"In that case," everyone agreed, "Heaven still has eyes."

"Of course Heaven has eyes," Chang Wen-an said with emotion. "If not, the imperialist aggressors would have conquered the whole world long ago. Let me tell you," he said with upraised arm, "there are, after all, more good people in the world than evil ones. I have met many good men at the front, so many. It seems as if all the good men are at the front. Though wicked people may be having their day now, they will not be able to escape Heaven's retribution in the end. If they do, their children will not."

Chang Wen-an spoke with so much force and conviction that

he appeared exhausted. He wiped the sweat off his forehead, smiled and spoke no more.

It was hot and sultry that afternoon. The sky looked like a sheet of gray cloth that had faded unevenly. The road up the hill was not particularly steep but by the time Chang Wen-an had reached the crest his legs were heavy and his breath short. He stopped and looked wearily at the fields of grain on the hillside as he sat down on a rock to rest. It was cooler on the hilltop and that gave some relief to the stuffy feeling that had oppressed him. Then looking back at the road that he had just come from and the town that wriggled through the long, narrow valley like a striped caterpillar, the oppressed feeling returned. With a grunt of disgust he turned his gaze in the other direction. The road ahead was more level but it was followed by another hill and he must climb that before he could see his own village. His mother was probably preparing supper at the moment. A feeling of tenderness came over him at the prospect, but this soon gave way to a sense of shame. Although he knew his parents had not expected him to come back rich but were glad to have him the way he was, although he knew that they had no inkling of the surprise that he had planned for them and the purpose of his trip to the next town, Chang Wen-an could not help feeling uneasy.

He breathed a long sigh and looked again at the big caterpillar in the valley on the other side of the hill. As he recalled his bitter disappointment, he could not help feeling resentful. However, he had no notion of whom he was resentful unless it was himself, for he had been a fool, he had not been able to understand that caterpillar of a town there, let alone the great world outside from which he had just returned.

He did not resent Uncle Tung's jibes at his innocence at all. As a matter of fact, he was rather grateful to the red-nosed old man for being frank with him, for having taken the lid off the putrid sewers and giving him a glimpse of the true condition of things back at home. He was taken aback a little when the old man told him that his thousand dollars would only buy half of one leg of an ox, but he got over that quickly enough. What he could not easily get over was what Uncle Tung told him of some of the townspeople, of the wealth that some of them had amassed, of the things they did to amass their fortunes and of their extravagance and wastefulness. The stories shocked and disgusted him. He was disturbed by a host of perplexing thoughts, and toward the end of their interview he only half heard what Uncle Tung was saying to him. Finally, he left the town and trudged up the road that led to his own village, his heart filled with bitterness. He felt keenly the shattering of his hopes and began to think that his return from the front had become senseless. The fact that there were actually such heartless people who took advantage of the national calamity to enrich themselves had, of course, something to do with his resentment, but if his cherished dream had not come to nothing he would not have been so despondent.

Finally he stood up wearily and started down the slope with a heavy heart. Then his steps quickened, for now he wanted to get home as soon as he could. He needed consolation now. But when he recalled Uncle Tung's words—"It will only buy half of one leg of an ox"—he became less eager. Unconsciously he felt the bills in his pocket. They were still intact, as he had found them on innumerable occasions in the past, but they meant nothing to him now. They would only buy half of one leg of an ox!

Chang Wen-an was soon past the bottom of the hill. A short level stretch in the valley, and the road woudl lead up another hill. It was shady in the valley. Scattered on the sunny side of the hill were thatched houses and winding through these ran a small stream.

Just as he was about to begin the ascent, a man came dashing down toward him and greeted him with obvious warmth and excitement. Chang Wen-an, however, did not know him. The young man's face was flushed and began to talk away to Chang Wen-an at a great rate. Soon the latter began to realize that the young man was Chen Hai-ching's son. He had been to Chang's house and had hurried to meet the soldier so that he could learn more about his father without delay.

"Ah, so you are Chen Hai-ching's son, eh? Your father is the man who joined the army with four pack horses?"

He caught something of the young man's joy and excitement. He forgot that he had not seen Chen Hai-ching at all, that he did not even know where he was. "He is quite a man. He is a hero," he said to the young man enthusiastically. "He is so brave . . . That's right, he is a sergeant now, sure." He answered the young man's question without the slightest hesitation, as if he had not himself made up the story for the benefit of the villagers that very morning.

Needless to say, everything that Chang Wen-an had invented about Chen Hai-ching had reached the ears of the latter's son. The young man believed every word of it, and because of his joy, he had spent the great part of the day looking for Chang Wen-an so that he could hear the story over again from the original sources.

The two men had by this time approached one of the thatched houses. To the right of the door was an abandoned trough for watering horses. "This is where we live," the young man said. "Please come in for a while, for my grandmother wants to talk to you. She won't be happy until she has heard the story from you herself."

Chang Wen-an suddenly realized that he was now the victim of his own white lie. What should he do? Should he keep up the fiction and elaborate upon it or make a clean confession to Chen Hai-ching's son? Before he could make up his mind, the young man had dragged him into the house.

He was immediately besieged with questions and expressions of gratitude and welcome. It was some time before he could make out the features of the old lady before him and the form of a sickly, middle-aged woman lying on a bed in a corner of the room. He answered their questions listlessly, only half comprehending what he heard. Again the feeling of a prisoner before the bar returned to him. Then collecting himself, he asked the man, "Who is the sick one there?"

"My mother," the young man answered.

"Almost a year now," the old lady said. "We can't afford to get a doctor and we have nothing to buy medicine with." She went on recounting her troubles: Their rice allowance was enough for their subsistence but it left nothing for emergencies. Then one had to have clothes. It cost as much to buy enough thread for sewing one garment as it used to cost for two complete garments.

"Mother's illness is partly due to her worries," the son put in. "She feels much better today after hearing the good news."

"That's right. Thanks to Heaven and Earth that he is all right," the old lady said, her wrinkles relaxing a little. "Buddha does protect good people. Mr. Chang, our Hai-ching is a very honest and good man, you can ask anyone. I am over seventy years old and have seen a great deal in my time. A good man always gets his reward some day."

"That's right, a good man always gets his reward," the sick woman echoed, as if in prayer.

Chang Wen-an had by this time fully collected his wits. He was cheered by the happiness of the three generations of the Chens but he was at the same time a little perturbed and he hardly dared to contemplate the possibility of being unable to keep up the fiction. He became fully aware what a terrible thing it would be if the truth came out. The realization made him resolute: he decided that he would continue to lie to the end.

He began to tell them about Chen Hai-ching, making things up as he went, faltering a little now and then. He boldly gave Chen Hai-ching a bright future and located him by division, battalion, and company, and named the place where he was stationed. The three generations of the Chens listened to him intently. After Chang Wen-an finished, they were silent and solemn.

Suddenly the grandmother asked, "Mr. Chang, didn't our Chai-ching give you a letter to bring back when you left him?"

Chang Wen-an started at the question. He began to tug at the end of his coat as was his habit when embarrassed. Then by accident his hand came into contact with the wad of bills in his pocket. An idea flashed into his mind. He had no time to give it a second thought, but with one hand pressed on his pocket, he raised the other much as an officer does when he wishes to command attention and said clearly and loudly, "I have no letter, but I brought some money from him."

"Oh!" ejaculated the grandmother and the grandson, and a sigh came from the sick woman.

With flushed face and quickened heart Chang Wen-an took the wad of bills from his inside pocket, still in the same oiled paper with which he had wrapped it half a month ago. Hurriedly he tore open the paper and began to run through the pile of bills with shaking fingers. But halfway through the pile, a wry smile flitted across his face, and with a determined movement he thrust the batch into the hands of Chen Hai-ching's son.

"How much is it?" asked the son, obviously impressed.

"A thousand," Chang Wen-an answered and then added with a wry face, "perhaps enough to buy half of one leg of an ox."

"Buddha be praised," the old lady said. "But how did he get so much money?"

Chang Wen-an looked around the room as if seeking for a suitable answer. His eyes came upon an old saddle hanging on the wall and he said: "It was given to him by the Government to compensate for his horses."

The old lady started to say something but she was unable to speak, as if choked with emotion. After a moment she said, turning to her grandson, "Didn't I say that sooner or later Heaven will reward a good man?"

The sick woman wept. The son stood transfixed with the bills in his hand.

Chang Wen-an sighed with relief, as if a burden had been taken off his shoulders. Standing up, he said, "Yes, a good heart always gets its reward sooner or later. You had better get some medicine with the money."

Chang Wen-an fled from the room amid expressions of gratitude of the three generations of the Chens. He hurried up the slope and did not stop until he was in sight of his own village. He rubbed his eyes as if waking from a dream and asked himself,

"What have I done?" Then unconsciously he put his hand over his inside pocket and said, "I can say now that I have disposed of the money that the commander gave me in a suitable fashion." Then looking back at the Chens' house he said with determination, "I must report the matter to the commander and ask him to locate Chen Hai-ching for them."

Whereupon he dashed down the slope as if on an urgent mission.

# $\mathcal{T}$he Red Trousers [1]

## By Pien Chih-lin

### I

All of a sudden the village of Anchü was thrown into a panic. The younger women at once took off their red trousers. [2]

The village of Anchü was only ten li from the Tung-Pu Railway, and had once before been visited by Japanese soldiers. In fact, it was only two months since the villagers had returned to their ransacked homes, which they had been forced to abandon during a previous raid. After their return they had hardly had time enough to replace some of the furniture which had been burned when suddenly one afternoon the news reached them that the Japanese were "pacifying" [3] the villages along the railway and had already reached the neighboring village of Lu, eight li north of Anchü. There, it was whispered, an eight-year-old girl had met with the kind of experience from which one of her age would have been thought immune. The excitement soon reached a climax when a letter which must have been delivered stealthily by some *hanchien* [4] was discovered at the village meetinghouse. It commanded the people of the village to wait quietly for the "Imperial Army," which would arrive the next day for the purpose of "paci-

[1] Translated by Yeh Kung-ch'ao; first appeared in *Life and Letters Today*, Vol. 23, No. 26 (October, 1939). The foonotes are Mr. Yeh's unless otherwise indicated.

[2] Worn by brides; they had to come off because they made the wearers more conspicuous and easier to spot by the Japanese soldiers.—C.C.W.

[3] *Hsuan-fu*, an obsolete Chinese term now revived by Japanese in the occupied areas, ostensibly to disseminate Japan's "friendly" intentions among the Chinese. A training school for such "pacifiers" was set up in Peiping soon after it was taken. The use of a "pacifier" to detect the feeling of the people before and after the taking of a city was a part of the Japanese technique.

[4] Literally, one who betrays the Han race; now any Chinese traitor.

fication," and if any villager was found to have escaped, the "Imperial Army" would not leave a single house standing in the village after its arrival. There was no longer any doubt of what was coming. Then, in an instant, the women took to the "modern" style: their long hair came away from the scissors at one crop, leaving something of a boyish bob on all their heads, whether they liked it or not.

Many of them even regretted that they had not loosened their feet before. But still the most noticeable thing in their clothes was the red trousers.

To the three-months' bride of Kwan Hsiao-shuan the taking off of her red trousers presented a practical difficulty. Hers were unquestionably the newest red trousers in the village, and though they, too, had been dipped and washed in the muddy streams in the ravine, their color had lost no whit of its loud brilliancy. What troubled her was not whether she should take them off or not, that no longer required any consideration; her question was what trousers to change into when these had come off. She had lost, amid the confusion and rush on their last escape into the hills, the parcel which contained all her clothes and a few pieces of Hsiao-shuan's. In the two months since their return, she had only been able to make up a few underclothes, a pair of shoes, and two pairs of socks, but she had not thought of the need of another pair of trousers, and much less of another pair in a less obtrusive color. She went back to her own home to see if any one had a pair to spare, but no one could help her. It was getting dark when she returned; and in the dimness of the oil-lamp she got on to her *kang*,[5] where she sat, alone and in blank despair.

Then Kwan Hsiao-shuan, to whom the afternoon had been no less gloomy, came home, and straightway the problem of the red trousers was solved.

Young Kwan Hsiao-shuan had in the early part of the evening exchanged a few harsh words with the village deputy and had

---

[5] A large divan-like bed, built of clay or brick against the walls and warmed by fire underneath. It serves as a bed usually for a whole family, as well as a place to sit, in most of the farmhouses in North China.—C.C.W.

come away feeling sulky and gloomy. When he entered the room and saw his bride still wearing those red trousers which had once pleased him, he seemed stunned for a moment; then, as if suddenly awakened to the sense of what he was to do, he slipped off his black cotton-cloth trousers and tossed them to her knees, saying dryly, "Change into them."

His wife glanced at him.

He quickly returned the glance and in a louder voice repeated: "Change into them."

His wife knew his temper well enough not to ask any questions, and the order was carried out instantly and without words.

They also exchanged their lined jackets: he wore her green and she was now in black.

The young wife, though full of curiosity and suspicion, dared not utter one syllable.

Tears came to her eyes when she saw that her husband was going out again. He paused at the door to look back and say gruffly: "Go on. Get to sleep. I'll be back tomorrow."


## II

Next morning when the first rays of the rising sun shone on the tree tops the "Imperial Army" arrived. There were eleven of them in all, but only ten horses, for the *hanchien* among them had come on foot. Before they appeared to "pacify" the village, they were conducted to the village meeting place by the *hanchien,* who ordered the village deputy to have tea served at once.

"The Imperial Army will not eat up any of your provisions," said the *hanchien* to the village deputy, "But," he added, "just fry a few *ts'ung hua ping.*" [6]

"All right."

"The Imperial Army will want nothing from you poor people," the *hanchien* said again, "only, while your people are waiting to receive pacification, let them find a load of cabbage."

"All right."

[6] Onion pancakes.—C.C.W.

"And also a load of turnips."

"All right."

"And look round for one hundred fresh eggs."

The deputy unconsciously knitted his brow; he seemed to border on doubt for a second, but quickly recovered and said another "All right."

While the ten horses were feeding on yellow beans in the open yard in front of the village meeting place; seven Japanese soldiers and the *hanchien* were gorging on the *ts'ung hua ping* behind the trellised paper window. But where were the other three of the "Imperial Army"?

They had gone out, it was said, to inspect the vegetable fields. When the seven had done with eating, the fat sergeant turned to say a few words to the *hanchien,* who immediately spoke to the village deputy: "Time for pacification now. Go and sound the gong. Collect the whole village in the front yard to receive words of pacification."

Exactly eighty persons turned out from the eighty houses in the village. Not one more. Half of them were children, who had been dragged out of their homes to make up the presentable number. One full shoulderload of cabbages, another of turnips, and a basketful of eggs were already on display in front of the village meeting place.

The fat sergeant stood on the stone steps and began to pacify in Japanese with the *hanchien* as interpreter. "The Imperial Army has never met with defeat. Never. It is invincible. We have come not to kill but to protect the Chinese people. . . . The dare-to-die corps of the Eighth Route Army are the most barbarous of your Chinese bandits . . . From now on you must report to the Imperial Army any news you may hear of these bandits . . ."

Then began a series of questions and replies:

"Does the Imperial Army kill?"

"No."

"And loot?"

"No."

"And burn?"

"No."

"Are you afraid of the Imperial Army?"

"No, we are not afraid."

"Then why do you choose to stay on when the bandits come, but run away when *we* come?"

Silence.

Realizing that he had given himself away by asking this, the fat sergeant saw it advisable to come to an end.

"The next time we come, don't run away. Hasn't everything been safe and sound this time? We never disturb the people."

Now they were ready to leave. The vegetables and the eggs were also ready, only they were still short of three men. The fat sergeant told the *hanchien* to ask the villagers if any of them had seen them, or knew where they had gone. But no one knew anything.

The village deputy sent some villagers to look round.

They came back after a long while with only, "Not a sign of them."

Then the village deputy himself went.

That witch of a slut of Kwan Hsiao-shuan's must have captivated all three of them with her usual display of bridal colors. Thus thinking, he pushed open the door of Kwan Hsiao-shuan's one-room house. There was Kwan Hsiao-shuan huddled and cringing in the far corner of the *kang*. Half angry and half inclined to laugh, the deputy said at one breath:

"Ha! Ha! the brave soul that you are! Never thought you would hide here like a woman! Come, where has your wife taken the three devils she has seduced?"

Hardly had he finished when he saw that it was no other than Kwan Hsiao-shuan's wife on whom he had been venting his wrath. Stunned by the discovery, he was too angry to laugh, and he retreated at once to start a house-to-house search for the "devils."

After looking into every house he came back, speechless with indignation, to where the seven soldiers had been waiting. He did not think that his failure would so soon draw down the wrath of Heaven upon himself. From a state of bewildered confusion he came to himself already roped to a poplar in front of the meeting place.

The village was in great consternation.

The excitement took on a new aspect when suddenly a group of villagers appeared at a distance dragging along an eleven- or twelve-year-old boy and shouting the while, "He knows, he knows!"

"You know where they have gone?" asked the *hanchien,* who was a humpback but had an air of genuine authority.

"I saw them chasing after a woman in red trousers by the East Path. They followed her farther and farther until they seemed to have disappeared into the hills. Then I saw no more of them!"

"The *hanchien* translated all this to the fat sergeant, who thundered out a volley of firecrackers at him which in the mouth of *hanchien* became:

"Find me the red trousers at once!"

The entire audience was flabbergasted.

But one head among the group suddenly turned and looked beyond the row of poplars, and uttered a few syllables; then one by one all the heads turned together to the south, like so many ears of corn bending under a gust of wind.

"Here come the red trousers," cried the group incoherently.

What they saw in the south was a person in red trousers running toward them in long strides (could those be a woman's steps, many of them wondered). The figure became more puzzling when it was clear that it was being followed by a small company of soldiers in gray uniform (certainly not the three "devils" of the Imperial Army). And they were approaching the village by a short cut through the woods.

"Here come the red trousers! Here come the red trousers!"

But without so much as uttering one syllable the seven warriors of the Imperial Army at once mounted their steeds and galloped away to the north, leaving behind them all the cabbages, turnips, and eggs, besides three 38-caliber rifles and three horses into the bargain. The *hanchien* had also rushed for a horse but after having tried twice in rapid succession to get into the saddle and failed (the horse being too tall for him), took to his heels in a flurry and ran after the dust of the trampling horses.

### III

Soon the red trousers and their followers arrived but, alas! those who had wanted to find the red trousers had run.

But the humpbacked *hanchien* did not get away after all. He was overtaken in no time by young Kwan Pei-sui, another of the Kwans of the village.

The person in red trousers was no other than Kwan Hsiao-shuan himself. He had had no time to change into anything else.

"Well, these vegetables and eggs are just what we want to give the guerrillas." Kwan Hsiao-shuan stepped forward to address his fellow villagers. "But do you think we can still go on living in this village?"

"No."

"What shall we do then?"

"Quite simple, let's go into the hills and join the guerrillas. But leave nothing behind."

"Let's go," responded the crowd, which had quickly increased to about five hundred.

Within an hour, a long line began to stream slowly into the hills. Intermingled with men on foot were mules, cows, water buffaloes, and donkeys, carrying all the movable furniture of the village and the women and children, who held in their laps parcels, bundles, hens, and new-farrowed pigs.

Kwan Hsiao-shuan and his wife walked side by side. From a distance they were unmistakably a man and a woman, though one might easily mistake the one for the other, for they had not thought of exchanging their clothes.

That night, at the guerrilla headquarters a welcome party was given to the new volunteers. The commander specially summoned Kwan Hsiao-shuan before the gathering, praised his patriotism and bravery, and promised to recommend him for a reward for having taken prisoner the three Japanese and the *hanchien,* captured three rifles and three horses, and, what the commander thought to be most deserving of merit, for having strengthened the unit by leading the whole village to join it. When Kwan Hsiao-shuan heard that he was to be heavily rewarded, he screwed up courage and stammered: "I want nothing, just a uniform, sir."

The commander smiled good-humoredly, for it was just then that he noticed that Kwan Hsiao-shuan was still in red trousers.

A gray uniform was presently produced for him. When the meeting was over, he immediately ran out and changed into it. Then he shook off what dust there was on the green jacket and red trousers, and, that done, carefully folded them into a bundle.

With the bundle under his arm, Kwan Hsiao-shuan walked proudly to the mud-walled courtyard where the women were temporarily housed. They were to be sent to the sewing shop the next day. There he sought out his wife and gently dropped the bundle on her knees. Then nudging her shoulder with his left elbow and with a broad booby smile, he said: "Keep them for more peaceful days to come!"

# An Unsuccessful Fight [1]

## By Ping Po

The road ran through shrubs. It was formerly a small path, but the Japanese had made it into a narrow motor road, linking the town with several others under their occupation.

In daylight Japanese army trucks often passed along the road. It was still and cold at night.

Members of the Catch-the-devil-alive Squad—five of them— were at a point about three miles from the town. They hid themselves in the shrubs near a small stream not far from the road. They could see clearly any one passing along the road.

"We can see with our naked eyes every tree and every stone for ten miles around," the sergeant commanding the squad said with satisfaction. "Comrades," he continued, "when the enemy trucks show up don't bother them. There will be too many Jap soldiers in them, while there are only five of us."

Machine Gun wiped the sweat on his face with his dirty, big hands and objected, "Sergeant, why should we let them pass? Finish them; they are our enemies."

The sergeant lifted his eyes and explained, "If we were ordinary fighters we should doubtlessly finish them, but we are members of the Catch-the-devils-alive Squad. It is better to capture one alive than to kill ten of the enemy. We should remember what our mission is."

Machine Gun was not satisfied. He bit his lips in silence.

Other faces, however, beamed with delight. Like well-prepared students awaiting examinations, everyone was impatiently looking forward to the moment for the test.

[1] Translated by Chu Fu-sung; appeared in *China at War*, December, 1943.

Yuan Yi-ping, a primary school graduate, looked around and questioned, "Are we not to open fire?"

"We are," the sergeant replied, his finger on the trigger.

"What shall we do if we fire and kill them?"

"It all depends; maybe we will have to fight a bloody battle before we can achieve any results."

"Ha! so we are to open fire after all," Little Fang said and laughed. Two of his front teeth were missing as the result of a fall in battle two months before.

"Don't laugh, be sure to hide yourself well. Why do you lift your head so high, Little Fang? You want to get yourself killed?"

Little Fang blinked his eyes and crouched down.

"Look, somebody," Helmet broke his silence and whispered.

All five guns were raised. The sun was shining over the green shrubs. Two slim figures were limping toward where they were, carrying a bundle. Machine Gun cursed on finding that they were only two peasants.

The sergeant patted him on the shoulder and said to him, "Why must you talk? You may spoil the whole thing."

"What are we afraid of? The people are always good to us," Machine Gun mumbled.

"Listen, comrade, you have been a soldier for some time," said Yuan Yi-ping. "The people are of course good to us, but they do not always know what is going on and may betray us without realizing it."

"That is true," the sergeant said. "If the people should let out a careless word, our entire plan may be upset. It is a question of caution. Moreover, we have occupied a position good only for attack. It is difficult for us to retreat."

"Right," responded Little Fang.

"Don't make any more noise then," the sergeant ordered.

Silence prevailed.

Time was fettered on the back of a turtle. It was a long time before the sun was in the middle of the sky.

There was nothing on the road.

It is difficult to swallow dry food when there is little saliva in one's mouth. The squad sent one man to fetch water from the stream. Everyone drank like thirsty dogs.

The water refreshed the spirit of the group. Their legs seemed to have been paralyzed, however, after remaining still so long.

The sun now came from the west where there were fewer shrubs. It got hotter and hotter. The sergeant ordered two of the men to stand watch while the others took a rest.

Machine Gun went to the stream and washed his feet, humming a folk song.

"Say, Machine Gun," Little Fang proposed, "sing 'I Am Lonesome.'"

"I don't mind," Machine Gun said, "but the sergeant won't like it."

"It's all right, but don't sing too loud," the sergeant said, "and stop when any one comes by."

Yuan Yi-pung complained of the heat and took off his cap and wiped his face with it. The gray cap turned darker as it soaked up the sweat. His gray uniform was also soaked in sweat.

Machine Gun had finished singing "I Am Lonesome" and was beginning another song when they heard a truck coming. All five grabbed their guns and pointed them at the road.

It was an army truck fully loaded with yellow-uniformed Japanese soldiers. It came rolling in the direction of the squad, raising a column of dust after it. The muzzles of their rifles glistened in the air.

Quick-tempered Machine Gun lowered his head to take sight, but the sergeant held his arm. Machine Gun was annoyed as the truck rolled away.

Helmet, too, was annoyed. He said to himself, "There should be no such thing as not firing when you see the devils."

Everyone was angry. No one said anything.

The sergeant knew what was in their minds. "I know how you feel," he said. "Well, that is why it is more difficult to be in the Catch-the-devil-alive squad than in a regular unit. You must be patient. The time will come when you can kill as many as you want to, but now we are supposed to catch them alive and we must bide our time."

Nothing happened the rest of the day.

On the following day nothing happened either.

Still nothing happened on the third day.

A week passed without anything happening, and everyone was getting blue. Every evening when they returned to their straw hut they were as disheartened as if they had lost a battle.

"Let's change the place, sergeant," said Yuan Yi-ping sitting on a hard wooden bed slapping mosquitoes. "Maybe we'd have better luck if we tried another place."

"No," the sergeant said firmly. "This is not a bad place. A small group of them ought to be coming along soon. Then we'll have our chance."

"I don't care," Machine Gun said. "I am quitting. I enjoy the regular kind of fighting better."

The sergeant gave Machine Gun a stern look and then said, fanning himself with his cap, "We must get over the idea that we are out to enjoy ourselves."

"I don't see why we must capture them alive," Little Fang complained.

"Shame!" Helmet said, turning to Machine Gun. "You are nothing but a bag of straw to talk of quitting."

"There are reasons all right," the sergeant explained. "Our mission fits into a well-planned strategy. For one thing, we'll be able to gain valuable information from the prisoners. It will be bad for their morale. Then we can make them realize the wickedness of their militarists and maybe get them to carry our message to their people."

"That's right," Yuan Yi-ping said. "We must stick to the end. We must capture some prisoners no matter how long we have to wait."

Machine Gun was silent. It was difficult to tell whether he was angry or ashamed of himself.

It was still hot outside the hut.

"Attention!" the sergeant called in a low tone as his eyes peered through foliage.

All five guns were ready and all eyes were fixed in the same direction. A small group of human figures came around the corner. They were Japanese soldiers in yellow uniform.

"This is our chance, comrades," the sergeant whispered. "Be brave. Don't be afraid. Don't be nervous. Let's finish some of them first."

Little Fang had the sharpest eyes and counted them off. "Eight of them," he said.

Machine Gun jabbered with delight and then began to laugh.

"Don't laugh," warned the sergeant. "Look, they are approaching. Hide yourselves well. Let's take them by surprise. Each of us will take care of one."

The yellow figures were not in an orderly march. All wore leather shoes and carried rifles. Among them was an officer with a pistol and a saber.

The sergeant spoke rapidly.

"Comrades, take sight carefully. I'll take care of the officer. Machine Gun, you take the one who has a swinging gait. Little Fang, you take the short, fat fellow. Helmet, you take care of the rearmost one. Yuan, be sure not to let your gun go off prematurely. You take the man who is now wiping his brow."

"No, sir, I won't miss him. It is the fourth one I am going to get."

"Right, and we'll capture the remaining three alive. If not, at least one or two."

The figures moved closer and closer. Their faces could be seen now. The guerrillas became more tense, their trigger fingers ready. They were sweating profusely.

"Fire!"

The three Japanese who did not fall scattered in panic. One threw himself into the ditch along the roadside. The other two hid themselves behind a mud bank. They fired wildly.

The sun was still shining. There was no wind. The trees were motionless.

The sergeant reloaded his gun and said, "The remaining enemy will give us little trouble. They are all frightened." Turning to Little Fang and Machine Gun, he said, "You two climb over the hill to the left and try to catch them from the rear. Be quick and don't let the enemy inside the city hear your rifle shots, or they may send out reinforcements."

Little Fang and Machine Gun scampered off with alacrity.

Not knowing where the enemy was or how many there were, the three Japanese dared not move from their hiding places. They continued firing.

The sergeant sensed that there must be someone behind a mound not far from him. He trained his gun on it.

The top of a yellow cap rose slowly up. The sergeant fired. The cap bounced up and fell.

"Two more left," Helmet said, looking approvingly at the sergeant.

Firing was heard from behind the enemy positions.

"Surrender, our Japanese brothers. We treat prisoners well." The sergeant shouted in broken Japanese.

The sergeant and the other two men crawled on all fours and converged on the enemy.

Suddenly the two remaining Japanese rolled down the bank toward a marsh and dropped into a stream.

The sergeant saw their pale faces. They crossed the stream and ran toward the woods. A bullet whistled through the air and another Japanese fell.

"There is only one left," the sergeant shouted to his men. "Don't fire any more."

Yuan Yi-ping had crossed the stream and was running after the fleeing Japanese. The sergeant and Helmet followed.

Once the fleeing man turned to look at his pursuers. His eyes were glazed like that of a dead pig.

Little Fang and Machine Gun were closing in from the opposite direction. The sergeant shouted, "Comrades, don't fire any more. Get him alive!"

"Yes, sir, we'll get him alive."

"Surrender, Nippon brother. We treat prisoners well."

The fleeing man made no reply, but continued to run.

The distance between the Japanese soldier and his pursuers became shorter and shorter. The former suddenly turned and threw himself down behind a tree. He fired.

Yuan Yi-ping was hit. He fell with his rifle firmly grasped in his hand. The grass around him was stained with blood.

Machine Gun raced to the Japanese soldier, who turned hurriedly as he heard Machine Gun's footsteps.

Machine Gun hit him with his rifle butt.

The Japanese uttered a sharp cry and fell. His cap was soon soaked with blood.

"Why wouldn't you surrender?" Machine Gun cursed.

"You fool," the sergeant shouted angrily at Machine Gun. "See what you've done. You've killed him."

Helmet tried to help Yuan Yi-ping up, but found that he was dead.

"I am sorry that I killed him," Machine Gun said apologetically. "But how was I to know that his skull is as soft as a walnut shell?"

"We have failed in our mission," the sergeant said dejectedly. "It is not bad to exchange one life for eight, but we are members of the Catch-the-devils-alive Squad. It's a shame to have only dead enemies to account for."

# Chabancheh Makay [1]

## By Yao Hsüeh-yin

Look at that fellow! He's a regular Chabancheh Makay!"

In our workers' guerrilla brigade "Chabancheh Makay" was the commonest oath. If the commander hid his cigarettes in his pocket and refused to pass them around, we shouted, "Hey, Commander Chabancheh Makay!" Or if someone sneezed loudly and then wiped his fingers on his sleeve, we said sarcastically, "You, Chabancheh Makay!"

The lice and the Japanese devils were equally our foes. During drill periods we scratched and tried to crush the beasts under our clothes. But when we were off duty, that was a different matter. We would sit around a blazing fire, take off our clothes and hold them over the flames. Then our enemy met his end. The lice swelled up like roasted sesame and fell into the fire. Then we slapped each other on the back for our victory, shouting, "Chabancheh Makay, hurrah! hurrah! Nibble it with your teeth!"

In short, we used "Chabancheh Makay" to ridicule anyone and everyone, never caring whether the usage was proper or not. But there was no evil meant—we used it so often because it was almost the only joke we had. Without it our life would have been about as humorless and as dry as the winter hills.

We gave the name to anyone, but the original "Chabancheh Makay" had left our troop long before. And he certainly was an original. From the time this farm hand had joined our troop until he was carried off unconscious on a stretcher we counted him our best comrade.

[1] Translated by Cicio Mar; appeared in *Tien Hsia Monthly*, December 1938; *International Literature*, February, 1939; *Story*, May-June, 1939. The *Story* version is used here.

None of us could forget him. Even our commander treasured Makay's old pipe as though it were a love letter from his sweetheart. For Chabancheh Makay never appeared without his pipe; it made no difference to him whether there was tobacco in it or not. He would wander off alone and squat under a tree, his pipe in his mouth, wrinkling his brows and staring out over the rolling fields. Sometimes he would pull on his pipe automatically and then two spirals of gray smoke slowly rolled out of his nostrils. Standing around, we would ask him:

"Is it your wife again, Makay? Still thinking of the pale-faced woman and your child?"

He would flush and then stammer, "Why shouldn't I? It's been a long spell since our commander has told me where they are."

According to him, our commander was omniscient in all things; and his failure to tell the whereabouts of Chabancheh Makay's family could only be the result of his fear that our volunteer would desert to join them. But Makay did not always daydream about his wife and home—more often he yearned to return to the rich land.

"Look," he would point, "how thick the wild grass grows in the field! Eh?" and he sucked his pipe profoundly, puffing out the last part of his sentence with a great cloud of smoke. "The Japanese are the cause of that. Before, people could live and work in peace. Then the wild grass never grew so rank."

Cleaning out the corners of his eyes, he would bend over the earth and pinch up a bit of soil between his fingers. Feeling the texture between his thumb and forefinger he would carefully examine, taste and sniff it. Then he would nod to himself and murmur, "What richness! How rich the soil is!"

Chabancheh Makay never did succeed in learning even one patriotic song. One time he tried to sing in chorus with the rest of us; but as soon as he croaked out the first line, we all exploded in laughs until the tears came to our eyes. After that he refused to sing another note. He just smiled, the pipe in his mouth, his blood-veined eyes watching our singing lips. Yet he knew two simple lines which he had learned in his boyhood—and these he always sang whether he was marching or camping, whether he was merry or sad:

> *A poor widow planned from the city to run,*
> *But she always met wind if not rain. . . .*

That frosty evening all of us had rushed out into the courtyard. We crowded around our commander, trying to get a look at this fellow who had just been captured. The unfortunate human was securely bound and tied. His face was deadly pale and his body trembled violently. On his head was a brown fur cap and sickle and pipe were stuck in his belt.

Our commander was standing sternly by, holding a little "sun banner" (Japanese flag) he had found on the prisoner. We stamped our feet and shouted,

"The devil take him! Look how he's disguised himself as a farm hand!"

"Shooting's too good for the traitor!"

Somebody kicked him and he slumped to the ground and lay like a paralytic at the feet of the commander. Such a display of cowardice was too much for us and some muttered,

"Ha, ha! This fellow's nothing but a heap of duckshit!"

But our commander was unmoved by this shameless spectacle. He continued to look coldly at the traitor, determined to find out more information.

"Your lordship," the wretch pleaded, "I am an innocent man. My name is Du . . . Du . . . Dumb Wang! Everyone knows me by that, everyone. . . ."

"Is it your nickname?" I could see the hair on our commander's cheek twitching.

"Yes, your lordship. My father it was who gave me this little name.[2] He was not an educated man and he gave me such a name on purpose to ward off the devils."

[2] Chinese peasants give their children a temporary name, as uncomplimentary as possible, in order to ward off the devils and thus enable the child to mature successfully. When the child is grown and betrothed he is given another more flattering name.

"Then what is your formal name? Stand up and say!"

"I have no formal name, your lordship." Poor Dumb Wang was so perplexed at this that he sobbed, "My father said that a farm hand never goes to school, never sits in a lord's reception room and therefore needs no formal name."

"But what are you called?"

"Oh, Cha . . . Cha . . . your lordship, Chabancheh Makay!"

"Eh?" Again the hairs on his cheek moved, "What is it you lack?" [3]

"Cha-ban-cheh Ma-kay, your lordship."

"To whom are you indebted?"

"People used to call me that way," Dumb Wang flushed. "The name was given me by Smallpox Wang, because the fellow always insisted in his idle chatter that I was a good-for-nothing loafer."

"Ha! Ha!" We could contain ourselves no longer and everyone shrieked with laughter.

But the commander did not laugh. He continued to ask questions of the traitor.

"I stay in Wangchwang village," Dumb Wang stuttered, "in the Big Wangchwang, not the small one. Then the damned 'Northern troops' [4] came. They insulted our women and shot and beheaded the men. My woman said, 'Let's move away for all the others have gone. In a peaceful place we shall be more happy, even if we have no more than water for food.'

"So we left the village; my son, 'Small Dog,' my woman and I. Now she has not tasted rice and water for two days and her stomach is as empty as a dry pouch. Yet our 'Small Dog' still cries for her breast, though he has drained it dry of milk."

With this our bound prisoner dropped his head as two streams of tears rolled down his face.

The commander said in a low tone, "Tell me briefly, why have you that 'sun banner'?"

"Your lordship, my woman said, 'Know that in a war time

[3] "Chabancheh Makay" in Chinese literally means "half a cartload of straw is wanted." The character "cha" alone signifies "to lack, to owe, or to be in debt."

[4] Villagers of North China formerly called Japanese soldiers Northerners, and Chinese, Southerners.

such as the present one, we can starve and die at any time. But we must care for the child, who must live. Why should "Small Dog" die, who is innocent?' And so it was my wife said again, 'Go back to the village. Unearth some carrots from the field so that the baby can have food.' And I went back one morning to my village. But as I was drawing near, some accursed soldiers, with fur caps on their heads, started to shoot at me all of a sudden. I ran back. In our hut again, I saw 'Small Dog' sobbing on his mother's breast."

And Wang himself sobbed convulsively.

"Don't weep!" our leader ordered. "And you became a traitor that way?"

"The devil take a traitor! If I were such a man, your lordship, the heavens over me would fall!" Jerking his shoulders, Chabancheh Makay excitedly went on, "Some people say that the 'Northern soldiers' won't attack you if you have a sun banner in your hand. So my woman gave me the flag she herself had made, saying, 'Spare no time, go and return quickly.' Then I asked, Isn't it dangerous to have such a damned thing in my hand if I meet the 'Southern soldiers'? 'Don't be nervous,' she answered. ' "Southern soldiers" are Chinese like us, you blockhead!' Your lordship, why should I, being a Chinese, become a traitor? Damned be my woman who advised me to take the banner!"

He stared at the commander who was clenching his teeth. A few more questions and the officer relaxed and smilingly ordered us to unbind the prisoner. As soon as he was free, Chabancheh Makay blew his nose and then stooped to wipe his fingers on his shoe. I noticed at once that he wore a rather new pair.

"From now on don't call those Japanese devils the 'Northern' troops, understand?" The commander explained in a friendly voice, "The present situation is quite different from the past. There are now only two armies, the Japanese and the Chinese. Do you see what I mean?"

"Why not?" he nodded, "I am not a good-for-nothing fellow."

"Have supper with us tonight. After the meal you can go back to your village to dig up the carrots if you like. We have chased the enemy away. Take the flag with you and if you ever meet them, show it; but don't tell where we are."

At supper all of us crowded around him. At first he was quite embarrassed; but when he saw that we were friendly he became braver and soon began to eat voraciously. He emptied his bowl and even licked the bottom. After our meal, he hiccoughed, picked a bit of onion skin from between his teeth and tossed it away over the head of a comrade.

One afternoon, a few days later, Chabancheh Makay appeared in the courtyard again. As we gathered around the commander told us that the farm hand had joined our partisan brigade. We celebrated the news by loudly singing the "Partisan's Song." But Chabancheh Makay merely stood there and smiled from beginning to end, smoking his everlasting pipe.

At night I bunked with Makay. I asked him, "Why did you join our guerrilla troop?"

"Why shouldn't I?" he said gravely. "All of you being honest men!"

After pausing for a moment to suck his pipe, he added, "If we don't drive these aggressive devils out, we shall never be able to till our land again."

I burst out laughing. Here was a fine fellow!

"Where is your 'sun banner'?"

"My woman is using it as a diaper for my 'Small Dog'," he replied carelessly, as though it were a matter of no account.

And he began to tell me of his family. I found that he was anxious to repulse the Japanese because he could no longer work on the land as in the peaceful days. He had decided to send his wife and child to the rear with the other refugees so that he might join our guerrillas. In the course of our talk, I noticed that his eyes were wandering here and there about the room as though something were bothering him. I silently watched him, wondering what was wrong, but he continued to sit quietly smoking, now looking at me and then at the lamp. At last he became quite agitated, got up and went outside. In the courtyard he made water, coughed intentionally for a moment and then returned. Having knocked the ashes out of his pipe, he looked at me for a while, put his pipe under the pillow and lay down.

"What a strange fellow he is!" I said to myself. "In spite of his rough appearance, he is so gentle."

Partisans generally like to sleep with a lamp lit, when it is possible. Soon after Chabancheh Makay joined our brigade two strange things happened on two successive nights. One night a comrade who had to get up in the dark, fell over another fellow and broke his nose. Who had blown out the light? The next night we all were awakened by the sound of firing. Sure that the enemy was near, we rushed about grabbing any gun or sword we could find. When we discovered that it was a sentinel who had accidentally pulled the trigger of his gun, we were as mad as tigers and insulted each other trying to find out who had put out the lamp.

The commander asked each one who had extinguished the light, but no one would own up to it. I, however, had an idea as to the identity of the culprit, so I stealthily looked at Chabancheh Makay. Noticing my gaze on him, he suddenly turned pale. His legs began to tremble. The commander walked over to him. "Hell," I said to myself, "he'll get twenty lashes." By this time his legs were shaking so violently that he was almost falling down. But the commander unexpectedly smiled and asked him mildly,

"Do you like the life with us?"

"Of course I do, your lordship." He took the pipe from his belt and offered it to the commander, "Does your lordship like smoking a pipe?"

We roared at that and even the commander held his sides with laughing. But Chabancheh Makay remained calm. He rubbed his head, then scratched his chest. Nipping out a louse, he squeezed it and then bit off its head with his teeth.

Next day I took him aside and asked him in a low voice why he had blown out the light. He flushed and smiled.

"Because the oil is so expensive, much more expensive than

before. And," he scratched his breast, "I am not used to sleeping with a lamp. . . . Well, do you smoke the pipe?"

By and by he grew accustomed to our collective life. He became more courageous and lively. Sometimes he even commented on our common activities. He knew some bandit jargon, which he used now and then. For instance, he called a road "a line," a river "a ribbon," a cock "a pointed beak," the moon, "a stone" and so forth. He criticized us this way, "There are many words which are unlucky to use and should be avoided. When we were workers there was no harm to use these words; but now, you know, we are playing at guns."

He would shun such "bewitched" words, but often we embarrassed him by pointing out that we, as revolutionists, should not use bandit jargon. Although he did not agree with us, yet he gave up insisting that some words were unlucky. To justify himself he would only say humorously, "Being a farm hand, I am ignorant of such new ways." And then he would grow silent.

"Hello," I said to him one day, "from now on you should call me 'comrade'!"

He shook his head and smiled. He condemned my statement with a murmur, "We natives of Shantung Province used to call one another Second Brother, which is the most respectful expression."

"But we are revolutionary troops, do you undertsand?" I said. "Revolutionists should use revolutionary terms."

"Ha, again a new way," he replied discontentedly. "I cannot understand—"

"The word comrade means to work together," I explained to him. "Just think, we share a common life, a common death, common sufferings, and a common battle against the Japanese. Are we not Comrades?"

"Right, Second Brother!" he shouted joyfully. "We will fear nothing, if we really work together like 'comrades'."

One night as we were marching out for battle, Chabancheh Makay stealthily touched my shoulder and said in a low voice, "Comrade!" Then he paused, smiling like a child.

"Comrade," he put his hand on my shoulder, "are we going to fight the Japanese devils?"

I nodded to him. "Are you afraid?"

"No!" he said, "I have often fought against bandits."

And we marched along side by side. When I looked at Chabancheh Makay I could not help laughing.

"Now I've caught you!" I shouted. "You just told me a lie. I can hear your heart thumping."

He looked embarrassed. Turning the pipe in his hand, he stammered, "I am not afraid of the devils, never: otherwise, I am not a man. When I was fighting bandits, at the beginning, I used to feel my heart drumming, but after a few minutes I would be calm again. Second Brother, a villager such as I fears only the government tax collectors."

About a mile from the village held by the Japanese, we halted in a graveyard. Two comrades volunteered to go ahead to spy out the land. A small detachment went around and ambushed in the rear of the village, while the rest of us were to follow our advance guard. Suddenly Chabancheh Makay stepped before the commander.

"Your lordship, I know the 'line' well. Please let me enter the village first."

We were amazed at his words. For a moment our commander looked at him incredulously. "Do you mean that you want to spy for us?"

"Yes, your lordship, I have had a lot of experience in attacking bandits before."

Some of the men whispered behind the commander, saying that he was not fit for the task and could ruin the whole thing. But our leader spoke to Chabancheh without any hesitation, "Good! But you must be careful."

And he turned to me, "Go together with him; be careful!"

Hand in hand we left the dark graveyard. We heard some discontented muttering behind us and then the commander, "Never mind. He is a cautious fellow in spite of his stupid looks."

An arrow's shot from the village we lay on our bellies and

looked and listened for the enemy. It was strangely quiet. Chabancheh Makay whispered in my ear, "Those damned Japanese have fallen asleep. Wait just a minute."

He pulled off his shoes, tied them at his waist and walked toward the village, crouching low. I began to worry about him. I moved forward a few steps and hid in some willows. With trigger cocked I stared toward the village. Nearly twenty minutes passed. No news from Chabancheh Makay! Growing more and more uneasy, I crept forward. Near the shelter of the waterwheel I saw a black shadow slowly moving across the ground. A sound and my heart began to beat like a galloping horse. Aiming my gun at the dark figure, I yelled,

"Who is it?"

"Me! Comrade!" It was Makay. "Those damned devils have all gone away. I couldn't find a one."

I jumped out of the willows. "Have you looked through the whole village?"

"Every courtyard and house; but there was not even a human hair to be found."

"Why didn't you cough or make a signal to me sooner?"

"Well . . . well . . ." Chabancheh Makay touched my shoulder, stammering, "because I still wanted a rope for my cow. Isn't it a good one? When I was fighting bandits before, I sometimes took things from other people."

And he showed me the rope gaily.

"Put it down!" I ordered. "The commander will shoot you if he sees that!"

Chabancheh stared at me with disappointment. Slowly he unwound the rope from his waist. I whistled loudly and flashlight torches suddenly flared. Our comrades rushed in to the village from every direction.

"'Second Brother'," Chabancheh Makay murmured in a frightened, tearful voice, "look, I've taken off the rope . . ."

On the way back, Chabancheh Makay followed close behind me. He was silent as a child who has broken a cup and is waiting for his mother's punishment. I understood the cause of Chabancheh Makay's anxiety and so I promised him in a low voice not to report it to the commander. He sighed gently and presented the pipe to me.

I asked him, "Do you know why we should not take things from the people?"

"Because we are revolutionary fighters."

Silent again for a moment, Chabancheh Makay suddenly asked me in a coaxing voice, "Comrade, couldn't we profit a little bit by the revolution?"

"Revolution will do a lot of good for us as well as for many other people," I explained to him. "In a revolution we suffer to some extent at the very beginning, then we defeat the enemy and enjoy the fruits of our common work. If we succeed in driving the invaders out of our country, then millions of people will be able to lead peaceful lives. Shall we not also benefit some from that?"

"Of course, if we can live and work peacefully, we naturally also—"

"Then we shall have a golden time. And our sons and grandsons will be able to walk in the streets with their backbones erect."

From that time on he became a vigorous and energetic partisan. He did not worry himself with thoughts of his wife and child. He began to learn to read; each day he learned one character by heart, but when he had mastered about thirty words, he was badly wounded.

One moonlit night twenty of us were ordered to destroy a railroad and wreck a train. We had no dynamite, nor had we very modern weapons. Our plan was to demolish a section of the track and then to attack the military train when it was derailed. The Japanese held a village not ten miles away.

Although we worked with great care, we could not help but make some noise as we pried loose the steel. In the midnight quietness the sounds carried far. A shot! Then rapid firing!

"Lie down!"

Just then we heard machine guns. Bullets fell all around us, thudding in the earth. Ten minutes of this and the firing ceased. A train was coming down the line.

Our detachment commander knew what to do. He bound six bombs together and stuck them under the rail. "Run!" he ordered. We rushed headlong to a graveyard close by and fell on our bellies. Chabancheh Makay stood with his pipe in his mouth as if nothing had happened. Our officer pulled the pipe out of his mouth and shouted,

"Get down!"

"Bullets have eyes only for evil men," muttered Chabancheh Makay.

The military train roared down the track. Our bombs exploded like a blast of thunder. Dust, smoke, shrapnel and the train crashed down the slope.

"Hit!" twenty voices cried.

Again silence.

Then shouts of victory and the commands of our officer. In the tumult I could hear a melancholy song,

*A poor widow planned from the city to run. . . .*

We rushed out of the graveyard toward the wrecked cars. Immediately the machine guns opened fire. Makay was running ahead. He cried with pain and fell. We rushed on. Then the gallop of the Jap horses. And we retreated. Chabancheh Makay was still firing like mad at the enemy.

"Wounded badly? Can you still walk?"

"In the leg," he said. "I don't want to run away. I want to kill those devils."

He struggled against me but I got him on my back finally and ran with our men. Sometimes we both fell into a ditch. Bullets, galloping horses, and the load on my back seemed nothing to me then. I only knew I was running and that I must keep on running. . . .

Another bullet hit Chabancheh Makay during our retreat. He was unconscious. Back at our camp we revived him and found that it was only a surface wound. We put him in a stretcher to be taken to our rear hospital. He was very feverish and murmured, "Ha, ha, ha . . . Da, da, da . . . my cow, my fellow cow . . . ha, ha, ha . . ."

# Purge by Fire

## By Yang Shuo

Some ten years ago when I was still only a boy my family happened to live in a fly-speck of a city on the Kiaotung peninsula.[1] It was then that I first made the acquaintance of Keng Chung-fang, a teacher of English in one of the local schools. He had just graduated from one of the universities in Peking and had come back to his own district to teach for lack of something better to do. He was short and had a narrow, pointed face. His eyes were lacquer-black and very bright and mobile, and his gestures and manner of speech quick and staccato. He reminded one of a nervous, sniffing, and darting mouse and was so nicknamed by the students.

During the last ten years Keng Chung-fang had gradually faded from my memory and I would have completely forgotten him if it had not been for the story that I am about to tell of which he was the hero.

When the Chinese forces abandoned the Kiaotung peninsula and the Japanese landed at Cheefoo, the magistrate of the city to which I have just alluded fled from his post and the cowardly gentry made secret preparations to welcome the enemy. The reaction of the people in the countryside, however, was different. This was especially true of Chaoshui, a fishing town about twenty li from the district seat. There the inhabitants, known for their love of violence, were all out on the streets and talking excitedly about measures to be taken in the emergency. Among the remarks most often heard were:

[1] Shantung province.

"That fellow Keng is right. If we young ones do not do something to save the women and children, who will?"

"What is there to be afraid of since Kuo Chun-sheng is willing to lead us?"

Kuo was the richest man in town. He had been away to school and seen the world and was respected by everyone in town. He had a sizable store of firearms in his house, which he would distribute to the able-bodied men of the village when there was threat of bandit raids but which he would take back once the danger was over, for he knew that it was not safe to trust the people, with their love for violence, with guns. It was because of this that Keng, a former schoolmate of Kuo, had picked him as his lieutenant in the uprising.

The two men sat up far into the night planning their stratagem. Keng was confident of success. His plan of action was to visit the neighboring villages the next day with his townsmen who had already joined the guerilla unit and exhort them to take up arms against the invaders. If they could muster a force of five hundred armed men, they would be able to disband the "Peace Preservation Society" formed by the gentry in the city and set up a government of their own. Then they would be in a position to enlarge their guerilla army and meet the enemy.

"I think we should try to recruit men in the city too," Kuo Chun-sheng said. "You can't tell when the devils will be here. We have no time to lose."

"But we don't know of any trustworthy man in the city," Keng Chung-fang objected.

"How about little Fan?"

"What? Do you mean to say that you want Fan Ling-chih, that gangster?"

Fan Ling-chih was one of the most notorious wasters in the district city. His father was connected with the district government and he made his living by running gambling establishments.

"Yes, he is the one I mean. He knows everyone and will be a great help. We need men like him. Moreover, I have had dealings with him and find that he is all right."

"Perhaps you are right," Keng Chung-fang conceded. "Suppose then that you take care of the recruiting in the city while I work in the villages."

And so about two weeks later the Anti-Japanese People's Government of the District of ——— was set up at Tasintien, with Keng Chung-fang as the magistrate. Tasintien was situated at the foot of a forest-covered hill which served as excellent cover in case of attack. The guerillas made a raid on the district seat and after a brief skirmish disarmed the police force which was then taking orders from the Peace Preservation Society.

The guerillas celebrated their success with a feast at which much wine and meat were consumed. There was a great deal of laughter and rejoicing and as the feasting progressed there were occasional fights. Fan Ling-chih was very much in evidence at the feast. He went from group to group, joking and drinking with the men. He was popular with them and everyone clamored for him, their vice commander.

Presently an orderly went to him, saluted, and said, "The Magistrate wishes to see you."

When Fan went into the compound of the newly formed district government he was greeted by a group of about thirty men.

"Here comes little Fan!" they shouted.

Inside the office he was greeted as cordially by Keng Chung-fang and Kuo Chun-sheng, the latter being now commander of the guerilla forces.

"Do you know the people outside?" Keng asked him. "They are from the city and asked for you. They want to join our forces."

"They are mostly boatmen. Of course we'll admit them."

"I suppose we'll have to take them since they have come. But you must realize that we have considerably exceeded the quota we have set for ourselves. We have now over two thousand men, while we have planned on only fifteen hundred. As you know, we do not have enough funds and provisions. So you must not recruit any more men."

"We can always get more money from the rich people in the city," Fan said.

"We can, but there is a limit to it," Keng Chung-fang said. "We can't refuse the men who have come, so you take them and give them something to eat and drink."

After Fan left, Keng excitedly paced the room, elated by the unexpected successs of his undertaking. All sorts of people had rallied to his call: there were students both male and female, peasants, fishermen, carpenters, and masons. A great many of them had come at the instance of little Fan, who also managed to get a large supply of firearms.

The Japanese established themselves at Chefoo but did not venture far beyond its environs. Because of this, Keng's district was comparatively quiet. An occasional enemy plane flew over and dropped bombs but not much damage was done and few lives were lost.

Being a far-sighted man, Keng realized the importance of establishing contact with the guerilla forces of neighboring districts and securing the support of the provincial government. To accomplish these objectives, he sent this friend Kuo on this mission. The latter turned his command over to little Fan and went off the next day.

During the next two or three months very little happened. The guerilla soldiers had little to do. They wandered listlesssly around town or lolled lazily in the streets. Often they would get drunk and fight among themselves. Keng Chung-fang became concerned with the state of their morale but what distressed him even more was how to provide for them.

One day two delegates from the city came to see him and told him that they were not able to meet the latest assessments. "We have contributed two hundred thousand dollars in the last few months," they said. "There just isn't any money left in the city."

What they said was true, for it was obviously impossible for a small district to support an army of over two thousand men, especially when they were fed on rice and pork. It was Kuo Chun-sheng's idea that they should be fed well, since they were to risk their lives against the enemy; he did not think what this would mean in terms of money.

Keng decided that the situation must be remedied. He went to see little Fan. It was almost ten when he arrived at Fan's quarters but the latter had just got up and was carefully brushing his teeth. Keng went straight to the point: "We have been far too extravagant," he said. "Our funds are giving out."

Little Fan did not answer immediately but went on with his morning toilet. Keng noted with distaste the expensive ring he was wearing and decided that there must be some truth to the rumors he had been hearing about Fan.

"Haven't we just made another asssessment?" Fan said finally.

"That's beside the point," Keng said. "We must practice economy as a matter of policy. Otherwise, we shall soon run out of funds again even if we raise another two hundred thousand."

"How are we to economize, may I ask?" Little Fan said with an insolent sneer.

"I want you to tell the comrades[2] that from tomorrow on we must all eat millet and vegetables like the *laopeihsing*."[3]

"Do as you like! Only I can't tell the comrades that. Do you want to know why? Well, let me ask you first why they have joined the guerilla army."

"Because they want to protect their own homes, of course."

"That may be, but I had to promise them good eats before they would come."

"Do you mean to tell me that you bribed your recruits with such promises?" Keng said indignantly.

"Say what you like. The only thing I know is that no one would risk his life for nothing."

"I don't care what you say but I insist that the food be changed tomorrow."

With this Keng turned around and walked out of the room.

"I must warn you that the comrades are armed and that I shall not be responsible if anything should happen."

Keng ignored the implied threat.

---

[2] *Tung-chih*, the Chinese equivalent, is used both by Communists and members of the Kuomintang.

[3] Common folk.

Something did happen, not, however, on the day the food was changed but about two weeks later when Kuo Chun-sheng returned from his mission. He was telling Keng about the tactical agreement he had made with the guerillas in Muping and of his interviews with Shen Hung-lieh, chairman of the Shantung provincial government, when they suddenly heard a commotion outside.

They rushed out to investigate and found a shouting mob gathered before the gate. The shouting grew in intensity at their appearance.

"Down with those two! We want Fan Ling-chih to lead us!"

"We want meat and rice! We want wine!"

Keng Chung-fang raised his arms to command silence but it was useless. The mob kept shouting their demands. Keng's face flushed with anger. He shouted at them, "Are you guerilla soldiers or bandits?"

"You are the bandit," some one shouted back, and it was immediately taken up by others. Then some one fired a shot into the air and cried with an oath, "Let's give the son of a dog a beating!"

Suddenly the oaths and threats changed to shouts of approval as little Fan weaved his way through the crowd.

"Here comes Commander Fan," the men shouted. "We want him to speak for us!"

Fan walked up the steps and motioned for silence. He was instantly obeyed. Then he turned around and spoke to Keng Chung-fang challengingly, "What do you propose to do now, Magistrate?"

Keng did not, however, answer him. Instead, he took advantage of the momentary silence to address the men.

"Comrades," he said, "we are all guerilla soldiers who have joined hands to protect our own people, not to oppress them. I can appreciate your desire for better food. We all would like to have rice and meat instead of millet and vegetables. But our people have to supply these things and they just can't afford it. And what do you think I have been eating myself? The same things you do. We must all suffer and work together, else how do we expect to fight the devils? Another thing, why are you against Commander Kuo? If he has made any mistakes you should point them out and let him make amends. Now tell me, what has he done?"

No one spoke up and Keng Chung-fang continued: "Since you, comrades, seem to agree with me, I ask you to disperse now. It has been due to some misunderstanding. Let us forget the whole thing . . ."

The mob, which had collected at the instigation of little Fan, began to waver. Men in the back of the crowd actually started to walk away. Little Fan, however, would not give up so easily.

"Speak up, comrades," he shouted. "There is nothing to be afraid of . . ." But before he could finish the sentence Kuo Chun-sheng had seized him by the collar and struck him in the face.

"So you, Turtle Egg, are at the bottom of this," Kuo muttered, but he in turn had to stop, for little Fan pulled out his pistol and stuck it against his ribs.

"Take your hand off me or I'll shoot you down," he snarled, and turning to the men he shouted, "Comrades, don't believe them! Don't you know yet who your real friend is? What did you come for? Speak up! Don't be afraid! I'll see to it that you get what's coming to you."

The mob took courage and again shouted their demands.

"We want rice and meat! We want wine!"

"Down with Kuo Chun-sheng! Throw the son of a dog out!"

The mob got what it wanted. Rice and pork were served again and wine. That same night Kuo Chun-sheng quietly slipped out of town.

Keng Chung-fang was apparently broken by the experience. He played deaf and dumb to everything and did nothing to check little Fan's acts of extortion. Once Fan's men intercepted and arrested a small merchant who had come back from Shanghai. He was accused of being a Japanese spy and mercilessly beaten. Later the man was able to establish his innocence but the fifty dollars he was carrying with him and which Fan had confiscated was never returned to him. So oppressive Fan became that the collaborationist gentry secretly wired to the Japanese at Chefoo and asked them to send an army of deliverance, which, however, never came, as the Japanese were not in a position to extend their control.

Disaffection against Fan was felt even in the guerilla ranks. When a group of student guerillas came to complain to Keng Chung-fang, the latter only sighed and professed helplessness.

"What can I do," he said, "since he is in control? I am in danger of my own life if I oppose him."

"There are over two thousand of us," the spokesman of the students said. "Of these at least five hundred are good men. Of the remaining fifteen hundred not more than five hundred are Fan's men. You, Mr. Magistrate, must do something to save those of us who want to fight for our country."

"You are right," Keng suddenly lowered his voice and confided. "But you must be patient and wait for your opportunity. In the meantime, you should try to win to our side the indifferent ones. The day of reckoning is not too far off."

The day of reckoning came on July 18, 1938. At around ten o'clock on the evening of that day, little Fan had just finished his opium pipe and was preparing to go to bed when there came a knock at his gate. He heard his orderly go to the gate and heard him come back followed by the footsteps of another man.

"Have you gone to bed, Commander?" the orderly asked through the window. "The magistrate is here to see you."

"Not yet," Fan answered as he went to open the door. As he stepped aside to let Keng enter, he wondered what the latter was up to.

"What emergency has brought you here at this hour, Mr. Magistrate?" he asked, after they had sat down across a table.

"I have just received reports that some people are planning to liquidate our army."

"Who? Those pigs in the city?"

"That I do not know, but some one saw a large detachment of troops marching toward Tasintien. Maybe they have already surrounded the town."

"I do not believe it," little Fan said, frowning.

"I have a written report on it."

"Let me see it."

Keng Chung-fang reached into his pocket but he pulled out a pistol instead of a report.

"Don't make a sound!" Keng commanded, his pistol pointed at Fan's chest. Backing himself to the door, he quickly closed and bolted it and then went back to the table and sat down opposite Fan.

"You won't dare shoot," Fan said calmly. "You'd never get out of here alive if you did."

"Don't I?" Keng said, laughing. "Of course, you don't know that your house has been surrounded by our men."

"Don't try to scare me. I am not a child."

"All right, then, let's see if you can be scared." So saying Keng raised his pistol and fired a shot through the roof. Instantly the crack of gun fire rose on all sides, both inside the town and outside. Before Fan's men had time to get dressed and reach for their arms, the gate had been rammed open, and the compound filled with loyal guerillas.

"Lay down your arms and surrender, comrades," they shouted. "Little Fan has been arrested."

Those who managed to escape capture inside the town found a ring of fire outside. There was nothing for them to do except to surrender. By early dawn the firing had ceased entirely and Fan's men's, except for about ten who had been killed, had been rounded up and herded into the compound of the magistrate's office. Fan was there among them, having been taken there under guard, and was without question the most dispirited of the lot.

Presently Keng arrived, accompanied by a man whom Fan had never seen before and by, much to Fan's surprise, Kuo Chunsheng.

"Sorry to put you in such a fix, Commander Fan," Kuo Chunsheng said, waving breezily toward the prisoner. The three men then sat down and Keng began to recount the crimes that little

Fan had committed. At the end Kuo turned to Fan and asked, "Do you admit these charges, Commander Fan."

"I do," Fan said without hesitation. "I am a man, I am ready to take the consequences. But tell me, where have you come from?"

Kuo Chun-sheng laughed and said, pointing to the stranger, "Let me introduce the vice commander of the Muping guerillas. We had to have his help, you see. Now tell us what you would like us to do for you."

"Do what you please," little Fan spoke with the contempt of a desperate man. "I am not afraid of anything. But I want to remind you that I did spare your life when I had you in my power."

Kuo Chun-sheng stood up and made a mocking bow, saying, "Thank you very much indeed, but I am sorry that the magistrate will have to decide what do do with you."

Unfortunately for Fan, the sentence the magistrate pronounced was death.

A week ago I received a letter from a friend of mine in the city I have alluded to. The events I have just told were taken from the letter, which concluded with the following paragraph:

"Since the purge by fire, our guerilla force has become a well-disciplined body known as the Second Route Unit. It now forms part of the Third Army and is under the immediate direction command of the First Route Unit of Muping. Keng Chung-fang continues to be the magistrate and is working energetically with Kuo Chun-sheng on the front lines of the war of resistance."

# Builders of the Burma Road[1]

## By Pai P'ing-chieh

Along the newly paved base of the highway which stretches through Szechuan and Yunnan and along the Burma border, under the bushes and the scrub pine, there extends a long line of huts. These are the houses of the coolies who are building the road. Before them huge campfires are flaring and human shadows move here and there in the light of the flames.

Duck sits before his hut, hugging his knees and staring stupidly at the long chain of fires. The scene suggests a battlefield. And as some educated man has told him, "Those who work in the rear also carry on the war." Duck agrees with that. Building the road is like fighting. He remembers the time when he and his fellow villagers, in the dead of night, killed the big trout in the Dragon Brook with their sharp, flashing spears. Then he recalls all the times he has guarded his bean fields against thieves during the long nights. He would pick a few green pods and cook them by the side of the pool at midnight. Or the village head comes to his mind, and he sees again this petty official carrying off his cooking pot in lieu of the house tax. Now he sees again, in the flames of the fire, the detestable face of the village head, his triangular eyes like a wolf's, a big red nose and thick lips!

He leans forward and stares into the fire with indignant, defiant eyes as though he wants to fight the fellow. Never before has he been roused to such a pitch of fury.

Uncle Hu the Third slumbers on in his hut. His pipe still glows in his mouth and as the last of the tobacco burns, the drying bowl rattles and awakens Uncle Hu. He sits up with a start, hastily

[1] Translated by Cicio Mar and Donald M. Allen; first appeared in *Story*, March-April, 1942.

sucking in the last of the smoke, and with the back of his hand wipes off the saliva, which has drooled down one corner of his chin. Then he crawls outside, undoes his trousers and makes water. He refills his pipe and as he lights it with a coal from the campfire, he catches sight of Duck, pondering like a philosopher.

"Brother Duck! Why don't you lie down and get some sleep? It's too cold out here."

"Oh, I like to sit here and think about things."

"Perhaps you watch for the wild wolves? Or think of your old mother? Chao the Second brought us rice from our village today, and what did your mother ask him to bring you?"

"Humph. A small cloth pouch. And what did it contain?—three coppers, three sesame seeds and three green beans. It's supposed to ward off evil spirits and the flying machines of the Japanese devils."

"Stupid woman! Who told her that?"

"The village head! He told every family they must buy such a pouch at fifty coppers each."

"I hope your Auntie the Third won't buy one for me.[2] My store of rice at home is almost gone."

And Uncle Hu the Third crawls back into his hut, rather out of sorts.

It is cloudy and no stars shine. The wind is blowing steadily down from the hills and it smells like rain.

Duck wipes the mud off his feet with the wet grass and then he too retires into his shelter. Their little huts are set up against a big pine tree. Uncle Hu the Third occupies a narrow space and Duck a broader one. Since Sanman has neither cotton pad nor blanket, he shares Duck's bed.

Sanman is a hard-working and generous fellow. He will spend all his pay at one throw. As soon as evening closes down he throws himself on the straw and begins to snore. Duck is small in size

---

[2] A Chinese villager never refers to his mate as "my wife." He always uses some such form as "your aunt" to express the relationship of the second person to her rather than his own.

and he huddles up at Sanman's feet to pass the night. The heavy smells of tobacco and hay fill the enclosure.

Uncle Hu the Third calls from his bed, "Where do you wear the precious little pouch, my stupid Duck?"

"I threw it away rather than have the squirrels gnawing my clothes to get at the seeds."

Uncle Hu the Third often dreams of how he would put the village headman in his place by inviting him to the camp. Here he would show him the great ones who have come from outside to direct the road building.

One day he said excitedly, "Duck! We'll be seeing great things soon now!"

Early the next morning, while the dense fog still hangs over the valley, they begin the day's work on the road. Ho Yusen, the foreman of this road gang, edges up to Uncle Hu the Third and begins to pull his leg.

"Uncle the Third, today we'll see our great official of such high rank! Three ranks higher than our district magistrate he is! This fellow Chen Tahsiu once happened to lunch with our district magistrate and he came back to the village with such a pompous face! He nearly frightened the villagers out of their wits. But you, my dear Uncle, you will see a Nanking official of the very highest and the most supreme rank here with your very own eyes. Then when you return to our village, will you still recognize old Uncle the Second as your edler brother?"

In truth, a high official of the government is expected this day to inspect the road building. And all these peasant laborers are fired with excitement at the thought of the approaching event.

Excited yes, but they are apprehensive about it all, too. Folks like Uncle Hu the Third knit their brows and feel a headache coming on whenever they think of such an official as the village head. These officials are fellows that require much preparation. You have to present smoked pork or baked beef before you can expect them to do anything for you. Uncle Hu the Third has a treasure—a long pipe carved out of a bamboo root. Every morning he smokes three pipefuls the first thing after getting up.

After that he carefully hides it in his waist band. Chen Tahsiu, the village head, has often hinted to Uncle Hu how much he admires this pipe—how fine the bamboo is, how tough it is with many knots, and what a deep bowl it has. Yes, but Uncle Hu the Third likes his pipe too and for the very same reasons. And this very fondness has grown on him so much that any threat to his possession gives him stomach ache.

Ho Yusen, the little foreman, pretends to great sophistication and learning. He thinks Uncle Hu a very ignorant peasant, who has never seen the outside world. He does not realize that Uncle Hu the Third, thirty years ago, saw a great mandarin provincial official. But Uncle Hu has an answer for all his jokes.

"Your excellency, Mr. Foreman! I know the reason! You divorced yourself from your yellow-faced village wife, went down the river to a foreign school, learned a few meaningless words, and now you are as proud as a water buffalo. If you really know something then take this shovel and build the road! You're always insulting us with your 'dog-shit, that's all you're fit to eat'—so now tell us what does it taste like anyway, since you know so much about it?"

At that everyone roars with laughter.

The supervisor, whose name is something like Tsau, is very fastidious and pretentious. His eyes are small like a rat's and he wears his hair long and oiled and brushed back slick in the foreign style. Hearing the coolies laugh he rushes up, brandishing his horsewhip that has never touched a horse.

"You laugh, do you? And what for, you lazy bums? A great official comes today and if your work is not done well, I'll see you beaten till you cry—*cry!*"

The supervisor has great difficulty in speaking. He squeezes the words through his stiff lips, now fast, now slow—every muscle in his long face contracted into an expression of intense majesty. Sanman feels quite uncomfortable watching him mutter, and he can hardly restrain a laugh at the end of the tirade. The supervisor's small eyes grow redder and he glares round more fiercely. Then he points the horsewhip at Ho Yusen's forehead.

"F-f-foreman! Look what you're doing! H-h-here are plenty of stones. Remove them from the roadbed and throw them down into the ditch at the side. Do it at once! You only know how to laugh with these stupid fools!"

This is too much and the gang cuts him off with guffaws and harsh laughter.

"Laugh! Let me see you laugh once more and I'll whip you until you cry—one by one!" He cracks his horsewhip in the air and then trots off indignantly.

Ho Yusen, the foreman, busies himself with the rocks and the rest follow. They drop their mattocks and set to, removing the stones. But Sanman simply piles his up to one side of the road like a wall.

Duck too is puzzled by this order, "Throw all the rocks down into the ditches."

Sanman puts down the stone he is carrying and straightens his back,

"Devil take him! Why don't we keep these rocks for the surfacing of the road? The trucks will be mired in the mud here if we don't."

And the others have been thinking too. They nod their heads at these words. But Ho Yusen, the foreman, is silent. His superior has so ordered.

Uncle Hu the Third is encouraged by the foreman's silence and he makes bold to say, "Yeah, after the roadbed is done, we'll have to climb down into the ditches and haul up all these accursed stones again. Son of a bitch! We'll all be humpbacked yet! Ho Yusen, be brave and speak up! Don't you see how foolish this business is? You're a cat before the mice, but a mouse before the cat. But if a man's right he ought to have a chance to speak. Why are you dumb all of a sudden? I don't understand it at all."

"No use quarreling with him. Pile the stones up here!" Sanman slaps his brown belly. "I've worked for four district magistrates, traveled north and south of the river. Though I've never worked on a road before, I've seen plenty of paving and tramped a lot of roads and I know better. Ho Yusen, my stupid child, address the supervisor with diplomatic words—I'll help you!"

The supervisor sees them talking again and starts for the spot on the run. But before he can reach them, the men have made Ho Yusen call out, "Director! Shall we pile the stones up at the roadside or must we throw them down into the ditches?"

"Certainly, certainly." The supervisor trots up panting, "Throw —throw them away down into the ditches below there. Throw them all down."

Sanman stares indignantly at Ho Yusen, so that the foreman asks once more, quietly, "Perhaps we should save the stones to pave the road. Shall we?"

"Shut up! This is a matter of engineering science. Close your babbling mouth! How could you ever understand the profundities of engineering?"

"Sure, I understand." Ho Yusen's face is pale but his voice is firm, "I have studied engineering science in Rangoon University and I have seen with my own eyes the construction of the Burma Railway."

"My dear foreman," the supervisor shouts, "don't quarrel with me because we're all working for our country. You know this Yunnan-Burma highway is being built to meet the needs of our war of resistance! You—you should know that the high official who is to see us today is a very careful man. He will notice every little thing: where a patch of grass should be saved, where the stones must be thrown away; everything has been calculated in his mind! Before the road was even surveyed and designed he had examined the place many times. We should not make him criticize us. The coolies at the upper section of this stretch are on very good terms with me. You see, they have given me many valuable presents; but you—well, I'm sorry—"

Uncle Hu the Third points his finger at Ho Yusen behind the supervisor's back and whispers philosophically, "Oh! Oh! Do stay with us. Since you're also an official you must help us. It's a calamity for two such great officials to quarrel this way!"

When the bosses have gone off, Uncle Hu the Third cracks his toothless mouth in a smile and says, "Other days that fellow has not dared to walk on the road, lest his shining hair, creamed face and Western dress should be stained with the yellow dust! But today! Today, he must come personally to see that no stones may obstruct the embroidered shoes of his excellency, the visiting high official. And there's no helping it, by God!"

Everybody laughs at that and Uncle Hu the Third turns very merry and brags of the time when he was eleven years old. He had gone down the Yangtze valley with his second uncle to see the world. It was the first of the month when the county official visited the temple of Chen Huang, the Earth god, to *kowtow* that there might be good crops that year. A gun was fired three times before the august personage himself actually came out of the official yamen. Uncle Hu the Third's ears were almost deafened by the great sound. And the gongs, the official banners which said "Make way" and "Hide yourself," the sign boards, the huge official silk umbrellas, the horsemen with swords, the *la-la* band with pointed hats who ran ahead—what glories there were!

Finally Uncle Hu warns the peasants not to be scared. "When you hear the reports of the gun, don't be frightened. The palanquin will still be on the other side of the hill! When you hear the *la-la* band humming like weeping nightingales, you must not laugh." Uncle Hu then pulls a very serious face.

Sanman stops breaking the stones and wipes the sweat off his face. He will not let Uncle Hu brag so freely. "Now your tongue wags again! According to what I know of officials, they haven't got any gongs, banners or *la-la* bands! What you describe are nothing but those old plays we see on the stage."

"I saw these things with my own eyes, thirty years ago!"

Although Uncle Hu the Third is almost fifty now, yet he knows that his sight is as good as when he was a boy. Uncle Hu is also a barber, and even now Chen Dahsin, the village head, still asks him, with complete confidence, to clean his ears for him.

"Do you think one can use rice for seed that has been stored for thirty years? I won't argue with you as I never saw your great official. But according to what my eyes have seen, officials, great or small, are only accompanied by soldiers; and you can determine the rank of one by the number of soldiers following him. In my time I have served four magistrates. And each had four big rifles and four small rifles behind him when he came out. Another thing—have you ever seen soldiers arresting a man in the hills? If he's to be fined fifty dollars one soldier goes after him; if the man's to be imprisoned then thirty soldiers are sent; and the fellow who's to be imprisoned for three years is arrested by the whole garrison! You can tell the rank of an official in the same way. And I'll bet the official who's coming to see us today will have no less than eighty rifles. The small rifles will all be seven-volley,, ten-volley and twenty-volley; the big rifles are all Belgian makes, seven by nine, and there'll be two machine guns to each company!"

Duck is lifting stones and dropping them down the bank into the ditches below. As he works he thinks of what this great personage must be like. The officials he has seen have not been very great—only the village head and the supervisor. These two are arrogant fellows. He thinks that if the official coming today is like this supervisor here, then he will be a mutterer too. It is likely that he never opens his mouth and that when he does he is so furious that he can devour people. His voice must be even louder than a broken gong or a cracked bell. Or if he is like the village head, then his eyes must be permanently turned upward, his mouth tightly pursed and his nose as long as a foreign devil's.

Now the men are all at work. They lift the heavy stones and dump them down into the ditch; then Ho Yusen comes running up, bawling, "He's coming! He's coming!"

All work stops; they drop the stone where they stand and intently gaze into the distance, their heads bent forward. But they cannot see a thing. A few minutes—and the supervisor comes toward them with an old man and three young lads, all in khaki uniforms. The supervisor is muttering for all he is worth to the old man and he waves his arms to this side and to that in great agitation.

Uncle Hu the Third sidles up to Ho Yusen and asks in a low

voice when the official is coming. Ho Yusen points at the old man with shocked amazement. "He's the official—that—that old bearded fellow!"

Uncle Hu the Third is bitterly disappointed. No gongs! No banners, not even a *la-la* band! Ho Yusen shakes his head sadly and whispers the news to all the men. Slowly the coolies gather around the old man who has come to see them. Duck is laughing in his sleeve that so many people should crowd around this uninteresting old man; while Sanman furtively steps behind the visitors to see where they have hidden their rifles. According to him guns are concealed at the stomach, on the back, in the sleeves, or down a leg. But he can find no signs on these youths, nothing but mud on their uniforms.

The supervisor passes through the crowd and whispers fiercely, "Listen to the instructions! Don't make any noise. D-d-don't make noises!"

Then the old man leads the crowd down to a grassy slope below the roadbed. He sits alone in front of the workmen; Uncle Hu the Third is gloomy with disappointment in the back row; Sanman squats by the side of a stone mason; and Duck, who is still curious, lounges on the ground in front.

The old man wears a thin, brown beard on his chin, and when he removes his hat, they see that his hair is as though it were covered by the early autumn frost. Thick lips, short stature—he looks like an honest peasant. He speaks in a friendly way.

"I've been greatly concerned about you. The work on the upper section was finished yesterday. But you—are you fellows tired? How many of you have been ill in this bad climate here?"

Every man feels his heart slowly warmed by the words of the old man. He goes on to ask if the food is not enough, and if the huts are too uncomfortable. And about this and that. At first they answer his questions one by one; but soon they are replying in chorus and sometimes a wave of cheerful laughter sweeps through the crowd.

The old man goes on, "We must be efficient and the work should be done as if for a contest. We must not waste our labor!

Just now I saw that you were throwing the big stones down into the ditches. How well does the foreman supervise the work? Why does he neglect his duty to direct you? Pretty soon we will have to use those stones to pave the road. Then won't you have to carry all those rocks up to the roadbed again? Then you'll have wasted half your labor."

At this everyone turns his eyes on the director.

Sanman blurts out, "It was the supervisor who ordered us to do that."

And all the young and brave workmen stand up as witnesses to the accusation.

"Dismiss the supervisor!" the old man says decisively and with finality. "These times do not allow us to make such mistakes," he continues. "Our resistance is also carried on in the rear. Think of the thousands of our compatriots who are fighting at the front! How then can anyone dream of personal power, or personal glory? Every drop of your sweat means that a stronger barrier has been erected to protect the life of our nation! I'm also a workman, a coolie and the same as you!"

What words! Duck wants to jump up and shout. But the supervisor falls down in a swoon and rolls on the ground as if in a fit. Uncle Hu the Third and the foreman go up to the old official and ask pardon for the supervisor. All eyes are on Uncle Hu the Third—for look! He has his old bamboo pipe in his mouth and doesn't even remove it when he speaks to the old man, though the wind blows the ashes into his eyes.

When the day is nearly done, the supervisor walks up to Ho Yusen and begins to chatter in his friendly way, "It's said that Rangoon University is very good."

"Sure, very good!" (Ho Yusen pretends to be a graduate of this school.)

"Where is the university?"

"In Singapore."

"And who founded it?"

"The overseas Chinese."

This is too much for Sanman. He butts in abruptly, "Don't

tell such lies! Have a look at the stones—whether they're useful or not!"

Uncle Hu the Third sucks contentedly on his pipe. After a while he knocks the ashes out on the root of a pine tree and then offers the pipe to Duck, saying, "Duck, would you like a smoke?"

"No, I'm sleepy!"

"Smoking keeps off the bad air here."

Duck has no answer; he rolls into his hay bed and is so sleepy that he even forgets to pull up the blanket.

"Aya! You village head—you dead dog!" Duck suddenly shouts in his dream and begins to beat Sanman with all his might.

The same old nightmare. Once when Duck was feeding cracked rice to his chickens, the village head had come to seize his mother's cotton quilt, under the pretext that Duck had not paid all the house tax. The mother had held fast to the quilt and would not let him carry it off at any cost; and Duck himself had become so enraged that he had cried. He had pushed the official back and begun to beat him.

Sanman yells, "Duck! Duck! Wake up! Wake from that nightmare. Why do you beat me?"

And Uncle Hu the Third rolls over in his dream crying, "Wolf! Wolf!"

Duck wakes up and crawls out of the hut—his head reeling and heavy. The sky is like a great sweep of blue silk. The stars are winking, and over the hills in the distance clouds are massing. Silver moonlight floods the whole scene. A gust of chilly wind brings the fresh scent of new-turned earth from the highway. Duck breathes in great mouthfuls of the sweet, night air.

From the hut Sanman calls with great concern.

"Duck! Take care you don't catch cold! If you do, you won't be able to try for a prize in our Rear-guard Defenders' Contest. And the new official wants us to do our best for our country."

# In the Steel Mill[1]

## By King Yu-ling

At twilight—Szechwan in winter is always wrapt in twilight—
the electric lights at the gates had not been turned on, but we
began to file into the factory. The others had already got the
materials arranged. The furnaces threw out long flames.

We loaded the huge crucibles with irons of various shapes and,
with great wooden-handled steel tongs, stirred the materials to
hasten the process of melting. When the contents of the crucible
turned as red as the setting sun, our hearts were greatly relieved—
we were through with this pot. Other men worked at the hoisting
chains, and the whole crucible was poured into the troughs of
earth and sand. The empty crucible was refilled and the same
process was repeated. Occasionally we got a chance to talk to each
other for a few moments. The job was not too monotonous.

After the production of seven crucibles we were entitled to a rest
period of one and a half hours. We were so close to the fire that
not only did our heads feel constant internal expansion, but our
eyes frequently raised the devil with us. The red crucible would
appear to be a warship or a vast piece of grassland. The sparkling
molten metal was even more deadly. We would see it flowing out
of the pot in various guises and colors, dancing, singing, beckoning. Worst of all, sometimes we would hear it giving out the
most awful cries. Accidents usually happened at such moments.
For why should Fang Jen-san, our friend, jump into a crucible
full of hot steel after working at a pair of tongs for a long time?
We couldn't save even a trace of him.

For one and a half hours, too, the pressure burner was turned
off. The place became quieter. We got our heads doused with

[1] First appeared in *China at War*, November, 1943.

cold water. Some went out to smoke and others lay down on the sand piles. We always talked about things.

Tonight, as usual, Peng, the talkative one, opened the conversation. "Lao San," he called rather loudly at the young man lying close behind him, "are you making any headway? You ought to work fast. When you succeed, I'll be your orderly."

Lao San looked around a little and then said, "Don't brag too much for me. Our foreman put his foot down. He said orders from higher up were that no one is allowed any long leave of absence. I guess it's hopeless for me to become a company commander in the army."

"Why?" someone else asked.

"Why? Our foreman said we are all skilled laborers at this job. No more old hands can be found, how can he let any one of us go now?"

"You should have told him you are going to the front to fight," said Peng emphatically. He thought Lao San was too good-natured and did not know what to say. If he, Peng, had a relative in the army—a battalion commander at that—asking him to go to the front, there'd be nothing but the front lines.

Lao San answered anxiously, "Of course I told him all that. But he said our work here is more important than fighting at the front! They would not feel the shortage of one man at the front now, but the productive capacity of this plant would be reduced by the loss of a skilled man. How can we fight the enemy without materials? He also said the reason that the Japanese dared to attack us at all was because of their material power, not their manpower. No, he can't let me go under any circumstances."

"Then, you won't leave?" asked Peng with a show of impatience.

"Well, I can't help it," said Lao San. "In times like the present I can't walk out without permission."

Peng was in an argumentative mood. He continued, "At any rate I'd go. To be a commander of a company you'd get a lot more pay than you do here. If by chance your outfit came through with a victory, who knows but you would be promoted to the command of a battalion. And . . ."

Peng's words were cut short by the foreman who was at the moment just strolling past the sand pile. The man must have heard the entire argument. He said, "Peng, don't you try to egg the others on. What are we really doing? Can we say that we are not helping in the fight? We work hard and one day we will see the sun. You know how much we earned in Honan before, now our wages are nearly doubled. The Government is not treating us badly. Why should any of us leave our jobs at this time? Don't you think I am right, Lao San?"

The smokers had strolled back one by one. The firemen heaved in more coal. The flames roared in the furnace, drowning out all conversation. Everyone took up his tool and went back to work.

Fires under forced draft burned with gusto. Bars, sheets, and odd pieces were thrown into the crucible, the inside of which looked darkened like the sky before a storm. But there was no storm. The black things began to change in color, gray, white-yellow, and finally red. Solids turned liquid. The flames, coming through thick walls of the vessel, shot up in bright bluish white and greenish gold. My eyes became fixed by this magic play of colors. The man beside me nudged me, I resumed work with my pair of heavy tongs.

With heat the hard metal was turned into pliant matter. We conquered like hunters over wild animals. The chains moved, the soft liquid would become hard steel once more. We were pleased.

The crucible received another charge. The solid stuff seemed never to melt without the assisting tongs. Steel would always remain steel. A lot of painstaking work must be added to a piece of steel before it could be useful. It must go through many machines and be transported a long distance by various means, ancient and modern, to the places where the demand for steel must be satisfied. We exercised care as we would with a child who was expected to have a good future. To hit the enemy; to destroy the enemy—that would be the reward for all our care.

I began my third charge. Suddenly loud cries came from the men around another crucible fifty feet away. A crowd gathered there. Curiosity pulled in that direction but duty kept me to my work, so it was not till dinner time that I had the opportunity to find out the cause of those cries. There was no need to ask any questions. The superintendent and the foreman walked into our dining room and made a complete report.

That fellow Peng was a traitor-spy under the pay of the enemy. In our Honan days he was already connected with the enemy's special service. He was clever of tongue, and a good worker. That was why he could remain under cover for such a long time. Recently, however, the factory had received information of his doubtful loyalty and kept him under close surveillance. The foreman was moved to search through Peng's things by his provocative talk to Lao San during the rest period. Reports of the activities of our factory, of its production capacity, and plans for destroying the whole plant were found among his belongings. The superintendent decided upon swift action. The cries I heard were uttered by Peng when he jumped into the crucible to avoid being taken alive.

It was a simple matter, but its effect was great. Everyone of us cast our memories back through the past months to all the things about Peng, his air, his mannerisms, and so forth. To be sure, he tried to foment a strike for wage increases, he induced others to commit sabotage. If he were not a traitor, why should he want to destroy the factory which supplied the army with guns and the workers with a living?

After this incident the atmosphere in the factory seemed to be charged with a new spirit. Everybody developed a new love for the tools, machines, and the factory itself.

The bell sounded again. The machines moved. Our crucibles were again enveloped in flames that looked like big flowers of red and gold. Fresh charges were put in and molten steel would soon be ready for casting. When we felt dizzy, we would sing at the top of our voices to break the spell. Twelve or even eighteen hours a day—what did we care? We were turning ourselves into hard steel, and hard steel was the thing which our country needed the most.

The furnace roared. We hastened to load the crucible. We knew that steel was the thing needed to fight against the enemy and to reconstruct the nation. Our parents gave us birth, the land provided our food, but steel protected us from attack. Produce more steel!

# Test of Good Citizenship

## By Li Wei-t'ao

The reports continued to be optimistic but they no longer had the lifting effect that such news once had on people. For more than a fortnight now the papers had not published any news of our reverses. The few retreats reported were always qualified by such words as "strategic," "planned," "to lead the enemy deeper into the trap," and so on. But these euphemisms did not halt the enemy's steady advance toward Nanking.

When Nanking came within sound of the enemy's gunfire, it was already a city without political direction. It was empty except for those too poor to obtain transportation to go elsewhere and officers and soldiers who had been ordered to defend the city to the last. As for myself, I was neither: I was a member of the volunteer first-aid corps.

Perhaps I was more naïve and gave more credence to the optimistic news reports than most people did, or perhaps my job aroused in me a greater sense of responsibility, but the fact remains that I did carry on until I was captured by the enemy. I shall not recount here the circumstances of my capture, as I have already done that elsewhere. Suffice it to say that I had, just before my capture, managed to discard my uniform and change into civilian clothes, following the dictum that one should save one's own life when death serves no good purpose. As I threw the uniform into a stagnant pond I felt a twinge of self-reproach, but perhaps this eagerness to save oneself is understandable, especially in view of the fact that many of those whose responsibility was to defend the city had already departed.

Nanking fell into a state of utter confusion after the departure of the officials and army officers. Reports on when the enemy entered the city differed, but it was around seven in the morning, the thirteenth of December, that I was captured at railroad crossing on Central Road.

My puny appearance was in my favor. In the ill-fitting robes that I was wearing I looked very much like a schoolmaster of the old type. The spectacles with strong myopic lenses further proclaimed that I could not have been a member of the Chinese armed forces. It was entirely due to my physical unfitness that I am alive today, for if I had enjoyed robust health I would have been slaughtered with thousands of others.

The captives were divided into three groups. The first group consisted of those caught in uniforms or armed. These were machine-gunned or bayoneted according to size of the group. The second group consisted of men who had neither uniforms nor arms to betray them as soldiers but whose age and physique made them potential soldiers. They were tortured and then put to death whether they admitted they were soldiers or not. The last group consisted of sickly looking men like myself. We were questioned not by the military but by civilian attachés.

Most of these civilian attachés were students of college age. They wore army caps and trousers but their coats were of the civilian type, European style. They seemed to have been organized into a distinct unit of their own. They were sent on short notice to wherever they were needed and were sent elsewhere as soon as their mission was completed. In the case of Nanking they arrived three days after the fall of the city and immediately set to work on non-military problems connected with the occupation. They were treated with respect by the army personnel and were addressed as *sensei* [1] by officers and enlisted men alike.

The man who questioned me was a student of Tung Wen Academy of Shanghai and spoke the Shanghai dialect quite well. He did not bother about asking the captives their names and

---

[1] Japanese reading of the Chinese expression *hsien-sheng* (Mr., sir); it is used by the Japanese to indicate a greater degree of respect than their native honorific *san*.

place of birth, for he realized that he would not get truthful answers. The first question he put to me was:

"Are you a tradesman?"

My clothes did make me look like a clerk or a bookkeeper in
a small restaurant and my first impulse was to answer yes. But
then I realized that I knew nothing of business and that I was
bound to give myself away if he questioned me further. So I
answered:

"I am a teacher."

My answer made him look up, for in his mind Chinese education was anti-Japanese and a teacher a highly undesirable
character.

"So you are a teacher!" he said severely.

"Yes," I said and added calmly, "I teach in the country."

"What do you teach?"

"The *Four Books* and *Five Classics*," I answered and rattled off
a few more titles of the sort of books that they taught in private
schools in backward areas.

"Very good! Very good!" he said, assuming a friendly smile.
"These are the best Chinese books, the best Chinese books."

But to prove that I was telling the truth, he commanded me to
write down passages from the classics. Only a steel pen was available, but I pretended to be unfamiliar with its use and held it as
one would a Chinese writing brush. He laughed and showed me
how it should be held.

I soon satisfied him that I was familiar with the books that I
professed to teach. He kept on saying, "Very good, very good."
Then he turned and spoke to a soldier and I was immediately
taken aside and given preferred treatment.

The trick worked. It not only saved my life but also earned
me many privileges. The other captives who were spared had to
carry water and ammunition and perform other strenuous tasks,
but because I was a schoolmaster I was given only very light work.
Moreover, they liked to talk to me through the pen, and thus
I was able to learn something of Japanese sentence structure
through their peculiar use of the Chinese language.

After a while they became quite friendly, sometimes even asking me to eat with them. Once a soldier gave me a sweater which he had taken from some unfortunate victim.

Thus in a little over a month I was able to make my escape and rejoin my colleagues in Hankow, much to their amazement.

# They Take Heart Again[1]

## By Lao She (Lau Shaw)

None of the three of them had any desire to play hero. Their age, their intelligence, their ideals in life would not permit them once again to drink in such intoxicating tales as the adventures of Kuan Yü and Wu Sung, though with these legendary heroes they had, at one stage in their lives, let their imaginations play. The mere memories of this hero worship in their childhood days now seemed repellent; indeed they would as readily disavow such experiences as they would deny ever having, in their boyhood days, stolen dimes from their mother's purses.

Nor had they the desire to turn renegade. Their age, their intelligence, their ideals in life would hardly approve of their kneeling resignedly at the feet of any master.

Yet there they were, marooned in a "lost" city. They could, of course, choose a path in between that of martyrdom and treason and behave like "ambulating corpses and walking flesh." Should conditions ever become unbearable, they could always drink themselves to a state of stupor.

Indeed, this path would seem to be the only remedy under seemingly irremediable circumstances. In physical prowess their joint efforts were barely sufficient to lift up a piece of heavy rock, and, granted they would heave it to a fair distance and by a stroke of luck kill one enemy, how much good would it do? Furthermore, intelligence would be a useless weapon for prisoners with hands tied behind their backs, destined for the execution ground. Never had they been in a greater dilemma!

Wang Wen-yi was physically the most stalwart of the three.

[1] Translated by Richard Jen; first appeared in *Tien Hsia Monthly*, November, 1938; also in *China at War*, October, 1943.

His one extravagant dream in life had been cut short by the rumble of enemy artillery; for one year more and he would have graduated from college. True, he could have remained in school and in time have been the recipient of a university diploma and a Bachelor's degree were he willing to subject himself to the rule of an alien empire; and he might even have an opportunity to pursue higher studies in the land across the Eastern Sea if he would stoop to renouncing his ancestry and his own race. He broke to pieces the small mirror hung against the wall—which a minute ago had reflected a pair of big, lustrous eyes, a broad forehead and a prominent straight nose—to get rid of the necessity of reminding himself of his existence until the day when the nation's lost ground was regained.

Now, Wang was seated with Fan Ming-li and Wu Tsung, classmates at college, though majoring in different subjects. Fan was not a weakling, though not as robust as Wang. His eyes were not any too sparkling, and his lips were thick. He resembled a middle-aged school teacher more than anything else. Wu was skinny, with a sallow, jaundiced face, and a narrow chest, looking slightly tubercular. But two penetrating eyes adorned his face and his voice was forceful and sonorous, compelling you to think twice before calling him sickly. Indeed he was lively in spirit, if not in body.

"What are your plans?" Wang asked casually, not expecting any ready answers, for he was anxious first to speak out his own mind.

Fan let his eyes drop, his mouth twitching upward slightly at the corners, a tacit admission that he had nothing much to say.

"Let's get out of town," Wu said, more as a question than as a suggestion, his voice less strident than usual as if restrained by shame.

"Get out of town?" Wang echoed softly, and after several moments shook his head. "No. There is no escape. Where can we go? And why? Isn't this just as good a part of our land?"

"I, too, have asked myself these questions," Wu explained, his voice a trifle raised. "I don't mean we must. Only, I think, it's not worth while for us to sacrifice our lives here. It won't do much good."

"You may be right," Wang said, nodding his head. "We belong to the educated class, and unfortunately our strength is infinitesimal, hardly of any avail. But . . ." he leaped to his feet, stood erect, and like an orator suddenly inspired was now speaking at the top of his voice, "there is no class distinction among slaves, college students are no better than ricksha pullers. Neither does caste matter among those who fight to free themselves from bondage, each one's life being as priceless as another's, and there is no rich blood or poor blood. If it's shed for the sake of the country he loves, the blood of anyone is equally valuable. Patriotism thrives partly on intelligence and partly on emotions. If we put our emotions completely under harness in our fight for national liberty, our intelligence will become the instrument of selfishness and aggrandizement. To think only of our own safety at a time like this is to have no sense of shame, and to stand aside from the struggle will mean the alienation of our people's sympathy. There is more in death than the hope of being made into a hero; don't think of martyrdom only in the small sense of being an extraordinary glory. It is our duty as well as everybody else's. The coward glibly talks about death being the easiest thing to do; only he who is prepared to lay down his life knows the true meaning of death. Escape is not for me, for my job is to concentrate my life right here. Death is valued not by how much it can accomplish but by the motive behind such sacrifice."

"I see what you mean," Fan agreed, his thick lips parting slowly, as if with great effort. "Death is not a matter of putting a quick end to life but of maintaining the undying spirit."

"This," Wang resumed, his brow flushed, "is not what is called heroism, but just plain, honest responsibility that goes with citizenship. While those who talk heroism are after an opportunity to cover themselves with a halo of glory, the responsible citizen has no other thought than to die with his fellow countrymen and be buried without so much as a tombstone."

"All right, then," Wu agreed, sticking out his narrow chest. "Whatever you propose to do, I'll follow you even to death."

"First, we shall take an oath."

Wu and Fan both rose after Wang.

"We three, Wu Tsung, Fan Ming-li, and Wang Wen-yi, pledge our lives to the cause of our country, to fight for its perpetual independence and freedom. Our bodies and our names may perish, but our spirit and justice and peace shall live forever."

"Forever and ever," Wu and Fan echoed in unison.

Their faces lighted up with smiles, reflecting an inward contentment that death was now to be the sweetest thing in life, sacrifice the highest form of beauty, and the blood in their bodies permeated with the fragrance of flowers. With tranquil hearts they began in earnest discussing plans for action. Now that they had found a solution to the most difficult of problems—death—there was no more necessity for gestures or speeches. It was time to make good use of their intelligence, for only courage with intelligence could help them reach the road that was eternally illuminated. They seemed to be hearing the soft, soothing beckoning of the gods, and they were steadied and unafraid. Some of the things they were saying sounded like beautiful vibrations, echoes of the summons from Heaven, and their heart chords were playing the seraphic music of national renaissance.

Permanently, it seemed, at the head of Lu-erh Hutung,[2] in winter and in summer, sat an old woman, spotless clean, as if dust and dirt had never dared touch her. Neither had poverty degraded her, for her aging eyes were eternally bright with cheer and friendliness, the sunbeams for all and sundry without discrimination. Though her eyes still served her admirably well, her hands were too shaky to do any delicate sewing, and mending worn-out shoes and socks for the poor was her regular profession. Her hobby was to flash a radiant smile for every passer-by, or to act as a sort of public reporter, particularly for grade-school pupils and ricksha coolies and give them such information as who

[2] That is, Lu-erh Street.

had gone south or north, or who had not passed by during the
day. All this she did gladly, and the only compensation was the
nickname Hao mama—good mother—which everyone greeted her
with. It was said by some that Hao was actually a corruption of
her surname, which was Huo.

For several days after the city fell, the entrance of Lu-erh Hutung was conspicuously bare, but the absence of "good mother"
had not attracted public attention because of the simple fact that
the people had considered it safer to shut themselves in their own
homes. Even if they had ventured outside, who would have paid
attention to her now? Compared with the loss of a slice of national territory, the life or death of an old woman became insig-
nificant.

But, finally, Hao mama reappeared at her customary place, in
the same environment. Her friends were carrying on as usual, the
ricksha-men still pulling, the vegetable peddlers still peddling, but
the atmosphere had changed with the appearance of the flag of
the puppet government and their faces were stamped with shame
and humiliation. She no longer had the heart to hail them as they
passed by. School children were no longer going to school; even
when they were seen sometimes quietly walking about aimlessly
on the streets with bowed heads, they were no longer singing
"The Volunteers' Marching Song." Horses and carriages were still
to be seen on the streets, but they all seemed to be part of a
funeral procession. Even the sunshine seemed cold and less
cheerful.

Through many turbulent crises and harrowing experiences she
had lived in her sixty-odd years of life, yet never had she suffered,
she thought, such burning indignation within her as she was
suffering now. It was crushing her, as wretchedly uncomfortable
an oppression as you would feel while dreaming nightmares with
your hands unknowingly pressing down on your chest. She had
seen tanks by the scores rumbling down the street, squadrons of
warplanes roaring in the sky, batches of rope-bound young men
and women of her own race escorted to the enemy camp to face
the firing squad, and larger groups of able-bodied men taken to

only Heaven knows where. The fury in her heart would not be burning so violently if it had not been invariably Japanese who were the authors of these heart-rending scenes before her eyes. Never in her life had she borne hatred for any man. She was illiterate and ignorant of national affairs, yet she had come to hate Japan like a plague. Her hatred was indefinable and inexplicable, save that in hating Japanese she vaguely realized she was after all better than an animal that cared only for three meals a day, and that she still had the capacity to distinguish between right and wrong. Now she knew that the monsters which roared overhead and rambled down the streets were all Japanese monsters, and that all the atrocities, massacres, and incindiarism she had seen and heard of were the handiwork of the Japanese. Yet no longer was she free to talk about the Japanese except in a whisper between her teeth. An acute sense of uneasiness and rebellion hung oppressively on her mind.

Most unbearable of all was the soldier sentry across the street, at whom she could never make herself smile or nod, full of good will for every man as she was. A long bayonet was forever attached to his rifle, gleaming in the autumn sunshine. His feet were broad and clumsy, and firmly planted on the ground as if he were afraid it might any minute slip away. But the place now monopolized by the sentry was Chinese land; this much she knew even if she knew nothing else more profound, as certainly as she knew that the piece of white cloth with a red blot on it was a Chinese flag. She simply had no desire to turn her eyes in his direction, yet that gleaming bayonet seemed to be blinding her eyes and those two heavy feet endlessly stamping on her heart.

Slowly the anomaly of the situation was beginning to dawn upon her consciousness. Why don't we beat him up, she wondered. Though at heart she bore malice toward none, she now honestly felt that to attack that soldier was the only right thing to do. Yet not only had the people not laid one finger on him but one and all invariably detoured just to avoid him. How weak-kneed these people were, she thought, how unmanlike! Had she a son and were he to assault that soldier, she mused, she would readily give him her blessing; and even if both she and her son were to lose their heads for that, her heart would still cry out "hurrah."

Gradually she came to loathe the place where she sat every day, yet somehow she could not afford to stay away lest she miss anything in case someone should attack that detestable creature while she was gone. So instead she found her attachment to the place daily growing, the soldier being the magnet. True, she found him as repugnant as a bedbug, yet her heart was pounding with the hope that soon someone would come along and knock him down. Perhaps it was her blood, filled with the strength of racial life, and her heart, saturated with the spirit of freedom and independence that had nurtured in her an antipathy to that man and an intense longing to see him dead. As for what benefit it would bring just to kill that one soldier she never gave a thought. It was enough that his presence so near her was a humiliation, and humiliation must be wiped out. As unconsciously as a young maiden comes to know shyness at a certain age, old "good mother" was suddenly overcome with shame, all for the sake of her country and national land. She wondered if a hero would appear to kill this foreign trooper; and a hero need not necessarily be a person with flowing red beard or an indigo face, but anyone among the many young men she saw passing by, if only he had the courage to strike that sentry.

She was waiting for her hero, any fellow who had a sense of responsibility at heart. Finally the sentry was being relieved of his beat, but the man who replaced him was no less ferocious-looking. The patrol was marching from south to north. Their warplanes were again whirring overhead, the two blots of red on their wings soiling, it seemed, the serene beauty of the blue sky. Our hero! Why hadn't he come? Wasn't her prayer, she said to herself, also the prayer of her people?

Thus for many a day she waited, but not sickened with despair. "How've we been doing?" she would ask feebly, but tirelessly. Occasionally a richsha-man or a peddler who knew enough characters to read the newspaper would tell her some news—though of Japanese origin—about the enemy's having occupied a certain city or nearing a certain town. Many of the names she had never heard before, but she would murmur: "What a big country we have!" And all the while her heart pined for only one thing. "Why don't we strike that fellow down?" she would say, pointing her threaded needle in the direction across the street as she mechanically did her sewing. "Wouldn't be such a bad beginning to kill one first."

"Sh . . . Good Mother," they would silence her, but triumphantly she would reply: "He doesn't understand one word of what we are saying. He's Japanese."

More encouraging news was brought to her ears one day when Wang Erh, a ricksha puller, asked her to darn a pair of socks which he had salvaged from a garbage can. "Good Mother," he began in a muffled voice, squatting by her side, "I was pulling a customer to the East City this morning, and when we reached the Ssu Pailou we couldn't pass. These dwarf soldiers were stopping all traffic. Two of our brave lads, I heard, had dynamited a trainload of their munitions and killed five or six of their soldiers." After stealing a glance at the sentry across the street, he quickly kept his up-raised thumb concealed inside his sleeve, meanwhile continuing in a whisper, "And they made good their escape too." In the afternoon, he added, he revisited the Ssu Pailou area and found the situation no quieter. "People told me," he related, "the two lads had escaped into a small butcher shop and then just vanished. Good Mother, these people truly have nerve, letting off those two fellows like that. We Chinese still have enough backbone in us, don't you think, Good Mother?"

Her face, after many days of solemn frigidity, now smiled with a spurt of pride. "If anyone has the nerve to shoot that sentry," she said, "I, too, will have the courage to do as the people of that butcher shop did today. Don't you believe me?"

"Surely I do," Wang Erh was quick in response, but kept his voice low with difficulty. "Given a gun I'd do it right now. What's the hurry, Good Mother? We'll get them some day, every one of them. When one has led the way defying death, pretty soon there'll be ten, a hundred, a thousand. Am I not right? Take the eel and the loach for example. Have you noticed in the fish market the fish dealers never fail to put a few loaches inside the wooden pail to keep the eels company? You see, the eel easily turns foul and sticky because it loathes exercise, but the loach is a lively creature, and soon there is contagion of activity. Our two lads are like the loach; once they start the ball rolling, they'll have plenty of people joining them.

"That's it. You bet, I'll be waiting here, and who can tell? Maybe tomorrow somebody will take a shot at him." Following the word "him" she once more pointed her needle at the sentry. "Would I die smiling just to see him lying there dead! I can't let that devil be my overlord."

The next morning found Good Mother sitting at her place earlier than usual and greeting every passer-by with a beaming smile. "He'll come," she assured herself after half of the afternoon had gone by without anything happening.

As she was about to call it a day a youthful stranger showed up, with a pair of big, lustrous eyes, a broad forehead, and a high straight nose. He did not look to her like a poor man though he had brought to her a pair of old socks. "No hurry," he said, staying her hands as she was picking up a needle to do the job, "I'll come back for them tomorrow. It's getting dark now, aren't you going home yet? I'll walk with you, and carry the basket for you."

"Is there a side alley inside this *hutung* leading out to the main street?" the young man inquired as they were turning into Lu-erh Hutung.

The woman shook her head and after sizing him up closely smiled an understanding smile. "I know you."

"What?" The young man's eyes were round with fright.

"You are a good man," she said, assiduously nodding her head in approval. "Now, look here. You see the tenth door on the south side? It has a back door, though it does not lead to the street. It's a private residence."

The young man said nothing.

"I can manage it," she said slowly after a moment of deep thought. "I'll tell the garbage man to open the door for you if I know what time you'll be there."

The young man's silence deepened.

"Your heart and my heart; they are alike," she vouched looking up at him.

"How do you mean?"

"I can't make myself any clearer," she chuckled happily. "But aren't you a scholar?" The young man nodded assent.

"Then you should understand," she remarked in a serious tone. "Now tell me. What time will you be here tomorrow? I won't sell you out."

"Tomorrow morning at eight."

"About the time when Chou Ssu comes to peddle his almond tea?"

"All right. When Chou Ssu comes that door must be opened."

"As you say."

"Do you know what I'm up to?"

"Yes, I know."

"What?"

"I know. Your heart and my heart, they are the same."

Arriving very early the next morning, Good Mother had sat there for more than a year, it seemed, before she heard distantly the sing-song cry of "Almond . . . tea." Her hands began to tremble and her eyes stared fixedly at the bayonet across the street. Then suddenly from a side street darted a dark figure, like a streak of lightning, behind a willow tree, followed by the barking of a gun, once, twice. The soldier dropped to the ground. While whistles trilled on the north side, and also on the south side, the dark figure had vanished into Lu-erh Hutung. But coming back to life and leaping to his feet, the sentry dashed to this side of the street, soon joined by many dwarf soldiers who had scurried over from south and north, like ants going forth to battle. After hurriedly exchanging a few words, the whole flock of them exploded into the hutung. It took away her breath. After an eternity, it seemed, the soldiers reappeared on the street, and when she saw no young man in their midst she heaved a deep sigh of relief. With her still shaking hands she picked up that pair of socks and resumed sewing without once lifting her head.

It was only four o'clock in the afternoon when she thought of quitting work, because her heart was turning too many somersaults. But before she had time to move, the shadow of the young man loomed before her. She could not believe her own eyes, so startled was she. He squatted beside her, busy in mock scrutiny of the socks she had just handed him, and asked in an undertone, "Did I kill him this morning?"

"He only feigned death," she shook her head, "for a little while he was as alive as you are now."

"Damn it! Next time I'll have to use a bomb," he regretted, drawing out from his pocket a dollar bill. "For you and Li Wu."

"Keep it for yourself, I don't need it," she waved her hand. "If you have an extra gun, let Wang Erh have it. He's ready and willing."

"Don't you worry, Good Mother! Plenty of men are ready and willing."

"What's your name?"

"For the present I have no name," he said, rising and stuffing the socks and the dollar bill in his pocket. "I may be forever nameless. So long, Good Mother."

"Be sure to aim a little more accurately next time." Once more the good mother's heart felt a great relief.

The trio was once again together, making an inventory of their work as well as shaping out the course of their future campaigns.

"The success or failure of our task," Wang Wen-yi remarked calmly, objectively, betraying neither elation nor disappointment, "is of no great importance. Its one merit lies in kindling the fire of the undying hearts. Our hearts and the hearts of numerous others are quite alike. We have only done our duty, and at best we've only marched one step further than the others. Well, let's map out our plans for tomorrow; and, striking while the iron is hot, we can turn this city into the enemy's grave."

# Portrait of a Traitor[1]

## By Lao She (Lau Shaw)

Everything that a twentieth-century Chinese can possibly enjoy and possess, Pao Shan-chin has been enjoying and possessing. He has money, a western-style house, an American motor car, children, concubines, curios, and books which serve as decoration; he also has reputation, position, and an impressive chain of official titles which can be printed on his visiting card and eventually included in his obituary notice; he has friends, all kinds of friends, and he has already enjoyed a fair share of longevity and health in a body fortified by varieties of tonics and stimulants.

If only he would allow himself to take things a little easier, to be a bit retiring-minded, he could rest wrapped in comforts. With his children and concubines to attend to his wants, life would be one effortless existence. Should he die at this moment, his wealth would more than provide for the comforts and pleasures of one or two generations of his children, and in the customary biographical sketch written for distribution after his death there would be enough poetic eulogies and lamentations to glorify his name. His coffin would be made of such expensive wood as to be able to stand against erosion for scores of years. And he would, of course, have sixty-four coffin-bearers and be properly paraded through the main thoroughfares.

But Pao Shan-chin would not think of giving up what he and most people in China call "a political career." His political career does not involve any policy, or political ideal. He has only one determination, that is, not to be idle. He could not stand seeing

[1] Translated by Yeh Kung-ch'ao, appeared in *Tien Hsia Monthly*, August-September, 1941.

other people in power and in the swim of things. He somehow feels that whatever he has no part in will eventually work against him; he must do all he can to frustrate it, or crush it altogether. On the contrary, he misses no chance of getting into something. Like a fisherman, he always makes full use of the wind with his sail in order to reach the exact spot where he is sure to make the biggest catch. It matters little whether the direction of the wind would work havoc to others; so long as it sets his own sail flying, he likes it.

That he has been able to sense which way the wind is blowing and to set his own sail to it accounts for the success of his political career. Once the sail is set right and has the full support of the wind, he will reap with the least effort what a politician in China rightfully expects.

Pao Shan-chin has no wish to retire. It would be doing himself injustice, to say the least, to let such foresight and genius as his go to waste. As he grows older, he becomes all the more conscious of the accuracy of his political foresight and the immaturity of others; to deny such gifts of expression would be absurd. He is only just passed sixty and is confident that as long as he lives and his facilities remain what they are, there will be political activity wherever he breathes.

He hates those who have newly sprung into political prominence; even recent events seem distasteful to him. The older he grows, the more he feels that his old familiar friends are the best. For the good of his old friends, he would seize every opportunity that comes his way. He seems to have a natural aversion to things new: new terms, new systems, new theories; and that makes him cling to his old ways all the more tenaciously. He is ready to co-operate with anyone, foreign or Chinese, so long as his "abilities" are recognized; for the same reason those who deny him power become at once his enemies. He admits that his "political views" are extraordinarily tolerant; and that in dealing with people he is at times unscrupulous and not entirely free from jealousy and prejudice. But why shouldn't he be so? All statesmen, he thinks, have been more or less like him. He is proud of the fact that he understands himself so thoroughly and that he is no hypocrite. Before those he can afford to challenge, he is capable of a kind of defiant showdown, expressed in a smile on his plump face which seems to say: "Be my friend, or be my enemy; take your choice now!"

He has just celebrated his sixtieth birthday, and his photograph appears again in all the newspapers in the occupied territories. This time it bears the caption: *Mr. Pao Shan-chin, newly appointed head of the Commission of National Reconstruction.* Glancing a few times at his photograph in the paper, he nods to himself complacently as if to say: "The old guard, they can't do without me!" He thinks of his past political career and the experiences he has gone through, all of which seem to lend weight and prestige to his present new title, which in turn will give him still more experience, more prestige, paving the way for even higher titles to come. For what the future may yet hold in store for him, he can't help feeling expansively ambitious. For over two years, his picture has not appeared so widely in the papers. To him, it is evidence enough that he is still going strong. New men may crop up from time to time but he, old Pao Shan-chin, is like the firs and cypresses, which grow greener, firmer, and more luxuriant with age. For him, the consistent formula has always been to have and to hold. There is no other way to get along in this world, and for the *kwanliao*[2] in China, this has always been and still is the golden rule to success. Pao Shan-chin never objects to being called a *kwanliao.* "Only people who can't find the way to be one ever call me a *kwanliao,*" he had said when he was forty. And he hasn't changed his opinion since.

Looking at his own picture, he feels that it definitely falls short of himself. The chubby face, the big eyes, the short beard, the thick, short neck, the barrel-like body, they are all there; but there is a decided lack of liveliness among those obvious physical traits, which doesn't do him justice. Like famous Chinese actors who know by experience which of their postures or movements will most frequently bring applause, he too has learned what manners

2 Literally meaning officials and officialdom, but often used in a derogatory sense.

and what facial expression of his own create the desired effects on people. He is not just a short, chubby, amiable person. He wishes that some competent photographer could have been given the opportunity to snap him in his two favorite and very effective tricks, which have become habitual with him and which he employs and manipulates with the ease and control of an artist. One is the facial expression which he puts on when he meets a new acquaintance or receives his subordinates: his big eyes will stare inanely for a momeint as if confronted with strange objects, while the flesh on his cheeks will first droop and then contract upward; benevolence will shine in his eyes until it finally melts into a smile; only then will he begin to speak, his tongue slightly curled to give a rounded and almost feminine quality to his voice, thus adding innocence to amiability. His second favorite trick is performed by his feet: his feet are small but thick, and he knows how to manipulate them to great advantage when he advances or retreats in the presence of his superiors. With his knees slightly bent, his feet will move forward or backward in short punctuating steps. The nimbleness of this footwork would normally be a source of danger to that bellyfull of flabby, slack flesh, had he not drilled himself to stability. As it is, his steps are not only steady but are able to express respect and humbleness.

To discover these two masterful physical movements in himself is to have discovered his inner self. To be in politics is an art, he often says, and these two tricks are expressions of his particular attainment of that art. He wishes that the public could be let into the secret of his success. But stupid newspapers are contented only with a simple photograph of a cheerful, chubby man.

Of course, it doesn't really matter. So many things, important things, are never known to the newspapers. He recollects how successful his last exhibition of footwork was! The chairmanship of the Commission of National Reconstruction had been seventy percent decided in favor of Wang Hsin-lao,[3] when Pao Shan-chin paid a courtesy call to Yamamoto and incidentally performed his

---

[3] The use of *lao,* literally "old," after the first or second character of the given name suggests respect.

footwork. What Wang Hsin-lao was afraid of promising Yamamoto, Pao Shan-chin offered with both hands: "You appoint me
chairman of the Commission, I'll appoint you High Adviser," he
said conclusively as he took leave of his High Adviser. It was then
that he performed his footwork, he backed out in quick mincing
steps, punctuating his verbal civilities with short pauses in his
steps and with his body slightly stooped. Poor Wang Hsin-lao, he
didn't even get a seat on the Commission. Stubborn as he is, after
all he is an old friend. "Yes, I must get him some position. Pao
Shan-chin never lets any of his old friends down. No, indeed." His
face broadened into a smile unconsciously.

Wang Hsin-lao was stupidly stubborn. Too stubborn. Yamamoto is an influential man; Wang shouldn't have offended him;
besides, to have him as adviser would surely make things easier
for himself. The Japs like to have power, but with subordinate
titles. This must be understood and reckoned with. To know and
to accept this means to have your political career here doubly
insured. Strange that old Wang should not see this after all the
experience he has had. He has been—yes, what hasn't he been!—
Minister of Railway, of Education, Head of the Salt Gabelle, of the
Customs, etc. He ought to know by this time that whatever job
you hold, it all boils down to the same thing: all that you actually
do is to submit to your superior with your signature the papers
that your superior has handed down to you. Why should he have
offended Yamamoto? Could he have some subtle scheme in his
mind? "I don't think so. I'd better nose around, though. Prudence
first! Does Wang Hsin-lao want to spoil my show?" He asks himself. He never likes to consult people on his intimate affairs, so he
often resorts unconsciously to soliloquy. "No, not Wang Hsin-lao.
Not he. No." The inauguration ceremony took place without mis-
hap. The newspapers said not a thing which indicated trouble of
any sort. Though some of the members of the Commission were
absent from the ceremony, they will turn up in a few days when
they see that everything is all right. Yamamoto was very pleased
with the ceremony that day. He invited all of us to dinner. The
food wasn't much, but as good as you'd expect from a Japanese.

So far, everything has been smooth, and with Yamamoto as boss there shouldn't be any trouble in the future. "Yes, I'd better do something to get Wang Hsin-lao a position partly because he is an old friend and partly to save myself the trouble of suspecting him all the time. As to the question of the understaff of the Commission, the rough outlines are already settled. The few recommendations from high quarters have already been taken care of. In the future, what jobs I can give, I'll give; whatever I can't afford to give, I'll pass the buck to Yamamoto. Yes, this time I can't complain of bad luck. No, I can't."

"I'll try to have Yamamoto's motorcar changed for a new one. Yes, I must do that. Japs like petty favors. It's time that I myself should have a new car too. But no, I'll have his changed first. Why should I be in such a hurry? . . . Why can't we both have new cars at the same time? After all, I am the chairman, and he only an adviser. No, go slow, don't be like Wang Hsin-lao! Better let Yamamoto have his first, yes."

This decided, there is no need to worry any more. If there is anything else worth thinking about, it is whether the second concubine's birthday tomorrow should be celebrated. She is too young to have a celebration party; besides, those who have failed to get on the Commission may get nasty and use it as a butt for malicious slander. If I allow no preparation to be made, what if some friends should turn up to offer greetings. A political life has this standing difficulty; it requires careful deliberation everywhere which can't be expected of ordinary people. In trifles as well as in grave matters, a slight slip leads to disaster. Take the matter of concubines; a man in politics simply can't help having concubines, but what troubles they bring! As for himself he has been singularly fortunate in this matter of concubines, partly because he has always had luck, partly because he is able to think out such matters for himself. Didn't he get rid of that Russian woman in Harbin with only $500? Yes, that was clever! He smiled conceitedly. "I won't have a foreign hussy again. Their skin looks white enough but how rough it feels when you touch it. Then, the odor on their bodies and those yellow hairs! I don't want to have anything to do with another one. The best concubine is still a middle-class lassie from Soochow or Hangchow, the Lin Tai-yü type, delicate and bashful, like my second. Young and pretty, she really deserves to have her birthday celebrated. Poor little thing, she has never been given much social recognition. Besides, it would provide an opportunity to ask Yamamoto to dinner; it won't appear so obviously for him. Yes, he will be the guest of honor. We will only have three or four tables altogether. I shall not mention anything of the birthday, and at the same time the little thing won't feel slighted. That's an idea."

Pao Shan-chin's happy destiny has brought him wealth and position which he retains by "his ability to think," a phrase he loves to use. His political and private life bears sufficient witness to this; Madame Pao has retreated into Buddhism, leaving him free with any of his concubines; the eldest son has a nice job; his eldest daughter is in college; the No. 1 concubine has three children; No. 2 gave birth to a girl last winter; and there hasn't been any family scandal, thank God! He never had much confidence in the morals of his grown-up children: what don't they learn in school nowadays! Fortunately, the eldest son has already got a good position and is soon to be married; as to the eldest daughter, he hopes she will get through college without any scandal and be properly married soon. The thing to avoid is scandal; politicians are never afraid of scandals but belonging in age and experience to the older generation, he likes to set an example to the younger generation; that is what one calls political morality. Being in politics one has to think of morality. The political stage is a place full of snares; without morality, you will be deprived of the courage to enter into adventures. At the age of sixty and with such responsibilities as have fallen on his shoulders, would he have the courage to forge ahead if his morality were a trifle weaker? No doubt, in the eyes of others his morality stands still higher than he is willing to acknowledge.

He doesn't want to look at the photograph in the paper any longer: it is nothing but a short chubby neck of a man, behind which lie the thinking power, the morality, the talent, the experience, and the luck of a statesman. He now feels like playing a few rounds of mahjong with his concubines, just to have a little mental exercise; his mind seems too calm to remain idle.

"Commissioner Fang to see you, Master." Chen Sheng quietly puts down a large-sized visiting card on the table.

"Show Commissioner Fang in." Pao Shan-chin likes Fang Wen-yu whose recent appointment to the Commission was entirely due to his influence. And he has turned up at the most appropriate moment, making up the fourth hand to the mahjong party.

When Fang Wen-yu enters, Chairman Pao remains seated. He knows that Fang not only will not feel offended, but will be pleased with this touch of familiarity. Pao Shan-chin's dilated eyes stare for a second, then grow smaller and smaller until rings of smiles appear on his broad face. Pao Shan-chin knows that this alone will more than make up for his not getting up. In fact, Fang feels patronized and flattered.

Such finesse pleases himself and makes him feel superior, definitely above Fang Wen-yu.

"Sit down, Wen-yu, sit down. I am so lazy. These few days have been pretty stiff for an old man, making calls and so on, you know." He doesn't want people to have the impression that he has been idle at home. He really dreads to be on the go, but he always likes to tell people that he is busy.

"Yes, I know that Shan-lao must be busy these days. I, I just—," Fang Wen-yu says apologetically, fearing that he has called at the wrong moment and appearing to want to sit down, yet not quite daring to take things for granted.

"No, sit down, you've come just at the right moment." Noticing Fang's embarrassment he seems to like this chap all the more. Fang Wen-yu will get on in this world, he concludes.

Forty-odd, tallish, pale-complexioned, Fang Wen-yu is addicted to opium, which throws an anaesthetic effect on all his other desires. To Pao Shan-chin he is a promising young man, smart, thoughtful, who has a style with him, but who unfortunately has never had much luck. After all the trouble Pao has taken this time to get him the commissionership, he hopes that he will get on to a wave of better luck.

"Wen-yu, you've come in time. I was just thinking of a few rounds of mahjong. I trust you've brought enough cash with you, haven't you?"

"I never knew that one had to fork out cash when one lost to Shan-lao at mahjong," Fang Wen-yu smiled, showing a few of his opium-stained teeth, but he doesn't laugh freely until Pao Shan-chin too chuckles.

"You have every right to say so, really. A member of the Commission gets only five hundred and sixty dollars, no carriage allowance, pretty tight affair, when you get down to it. But Wen-yu, you must know how to make use of your position, keep your eyes open, above all. When Yamamoto has formulated our organization plan, there will be appointments made for every district. You can recommend some, but don't just rely on letters of recommendation. You have to know the men you recommend personally. They will all have chances of becoming magistrates, you know. That will ease up your finance a bit, I dare say. Otherwise, you will lose money on the job with a salary of $560!" His eyes rest on the toes of his feet and he nods. After a short pause, he is jovial again. "All right, I will accept your credit this time if you lose. By the way, are you getting the stuff?"

"Yes, Little Liu brought me some real stuff the other day. He wanted me to try it first. Not bad stuff, of course, but the price is shocking!" He shakes his head, while taking up a Three Castles cigarette with nicotine-stained fingers.

"I also have some of it here. Not bad either. You can ask my No. 1 concubine for it. She takes it occasionally. I don't allow her to get into the habit. Let's go to the inner court." Pao Shan-chin is on the point of getting up when the telephone rings. He hates telephone calls. In fact, he never likes to handle things electrical, though he likes to have them round the house. It gives him a sense of authority when he makes use of them, such as telling the servants to order food or other things by telephone. It somehow adds to his prestige to have his orders carried out at a great distance. He has a sneaking fear of machines, and he knows that he is not one of those politicians who would rush about in airplanes.

"Would you mind . . ." he asks Fang Wen-yu diffidently, half standing up.

"Yes, gladly," Fang Wen-yu answers quickly. He takes a few long strides to the telephone, picks up the receiver, and smiles back to Pao Shan-chin. "Yes, this is Mr. Pao's residence . . . What? Mo-lao, oh yes, it's me, yes, you want to speak to Shan-lao, yes. But you know he doesn't like to speak on the telephone unless you insist. Oh, yes, I can take the message for him . . . Yes, yes, I have everything. Thank you, see you tomorrow, see you tomorrow." He gives the receiver a look and hangs up.

"Mo-shan?" Pao Shan-chin's jaw recedes while his eyes bulge, as if questioning.

"Yes, it's Mo-lao," Fang Wen-yu nods showing some unwillingness to disclose the message. "He wanted me to tell you two things: the first is that he will come to offer you greetings tomorrow on the birthday of your third *Taitai* and will be prepared to play a few rounds of mahjong here."

"What a capital memory! He never forgets such things!" Pao Shan-chin likes to have his friends remember the birthday of his pet No. 2. "And the second?"

"He has heard, it may not be true, that the university students will be out again to make trouble!"

"Make what trouble? What do they want this time?" His voice becomes low but clear, as if each word is an individual effort.

"Mo-lao said he had heard that they want to demonstrate against the Commission."

"Nonsense!" Pao Shan-chin sits down, his toes tapping the floor lightly.

Fang Wen-yu lights another cigarette from the burning butt.

"Of course, it's absurd. But I think we have to take precautions. Things have been going so well with us. We can't afford to let them come out, yelling and shouting slogans, and with those awful white banners like in a funeral! Don't you think we'd better notify the Bureau of Public Safety and ask them to send up some men to guard your house and a squad or two to each school to stop the students from passing the gate?"

"Let me think, let me think awhile." Pao Shan-chin's toes tap more quickly, the tip of his tongue sticking out slowly to wet his thick lips; his eyebrows remain knitted for a moment. "We'd better ask Yamamoto's opinion first. What do you think?"

"Good! Good!" Fang Wen-yu lets fall his cigarette ash on the carpet, his left hand slowly picks and squeezes his nose a few times, as if in deep thought. "But in any case we'd better notify the Bureau of Public Safety first and ask them to send down a squad of policemen in plain clothes but armed. It's better to be cautious. Let the men guard both entrances of the *hutung.*" The opium-smoker's face becomes lined with blue, bulging veins and his eyes shine with a forced glitter. "Yes, have both ends guarded. If necessary, they can open fire. I'm afraid nothing else can be done."

"Yes, nothing else can be done!" Pao Shan-chin appears just as upset, but is not so rash as his younger friend. "But still it is better to ask Yamamoto's opinion first before we act. If *he* wants to use force, our consciences would be clear; if he stands for peaceful measures, there is no need for us to stiffen up. I've thought out the matter. Tomorrow Yamamoto is coming to dinner. We shall talk over the matter with him."

"Shan-lao, I hope I am wrong," Fang Wen-yu says apologetically, "but what if tomorrow should prove too late? Even if we can discuss the matter with Yamamoto tomorrow, it is safer to have some men here first."

"All right, send for some men," Pao Shan-chin yields in a low voice as if in soliloquy. After a short pause, he seems not willing, yet compelled, to add something. He looks at Fan Wen-yu as if to make sure that he is the right person to impart this piece of confidence to. "Wen-yu, things are not so simple. You see, I can't go and discuss this matter with Yamamoto right away. The Japs always want to ask for details. If I speak to him about this matter, he will surely ask me who is the instigator. Just think, what can a group of ignorant young students know of anything; they must be incited by some people, the real trouble-makers. You will probably say that communists are behind them." He notices that the corners of Fang Wen-yu's mouth twitch. "No. No." He shakes his head decisively and with an obvious sense of revelation. "There are no real communists in China. I've lived for sixty years and haven't seen one single communist yet. Behind the students there must be other people. These people are not communists; they are the very people who want to replace us, replace you and me." His voice becomes louder and his face reddens. "We've got to find out who is or who are the people behind the movement, so that we won't be stuck when Yamamoto takes us to task. You see, suppose Yamamoto should ask me who is really behind the movement and I couldn't tell him, he will stare blankly at the ceiling and say sarcastically, 'Mr. Pao, don't you know who wants your position?' I can't stand that. As to how to handle our enemy, we can listen to Yamamoto, but it is up to ourselves to find out who our enemy is. Am I not right?"

Overwhelmed with admiration, Fang Wen-yu stutters, "Shan-lao, should I live another forty years, I doubt if I could acquire as much wisdom as you have shown. I wish I could see things half as clearly!"

Shan-lao makes no answer, his eyelids drop for a moment to acknowledge the compliment. "Yes, 'In capturing bandits, capture their chief first.' Once we get the instigator, the students will quiet down in no time. I've said we can leave it to Yamamoto to mete out the proper punishment as he deems fit. We'd better leave that to him, because the instigator, whoever he is, is probably no small person, don't you see?" In another moment he continues: "If we can't find out who is behind all this nonsense, Yamamoto can easily say, 'If you don't know who is the instigator, then we have to consider this as a mere case of student trouble.' That will be terrible. Think of it, we can't even handle a mere case of students getting unruly; even for this we have to beg for advice. We will not only lose face but invite trouble. You said, if the worst comes to the worst, the men will have to open fire and that will scare them away. But why should we be responsible for the firing? If Yamamoto is responsible, let him do anything he wants; he can order the guns to fire on them, if he likes. Wen-yu, don't you think I am right?"

"Most decidedly yes," Fang Wen-yu wipes his eyes with a dirty silk handkerchief. "But even if we did order the firing ourselves, what of it? Don't they deserve it even if they are some one else's puppets? What do they expect when they don't study and insist on making trouble? Our Japanese friends, Chinese friends, the merchants, the laborers, even the farmers will sympathize with us. These young idiots! We have to show them some discipline. After all the pains, the sacrifice, and the efforts we have made to set things up, for them to come round and shout 'Down with' to us! The impudence!"

Seeing Shan-lao nodding in approval, what little fire of indignation an opium-smoker is capable of subsides. "How about this procedure, Shan-lao? I will ask the Bureau of Public Safety to send down some men, while we try to find out by telephoning to different places who is behind the thing." Then his eyes suddenly brighten up, "What do you think of calling a meeting of the Commission?"

"Let me think it over." He doesn't want to appear completely dominated by Fang Wen-yu. From experience, he has learned that very often not to reach any decision is itself a decision, and procrastination sometimes kills both time and trouble. "Don't telephone to the Bureau yet. They should come to us first. It is their job and it is their chance to show off. Why should we go and beg of them first? As to the meeting, there is no need, I think. In the first place, the members are not all here yet; in the second place, not everyone of the members was recommended by me. To have a meeting under these circumstances may even create trouble for ourselves. Our first step is still to find out who the instigator is. When we get the man, we will pass everything to Yamamoto. We shall then spare ourselves the trouble and the mental agony, and at the same time we needn't offend anyone."

Fang Wen-yu is about to speak when the telephone rings again.

This time he doesn't wait for Fang Wen-yu to offer his services; instead, his plump little feet carry him in quick steps, like a duck wobbling hurriedly, to the telephone. He picks up the receiver and draws a deep breath: "Who is it? Oh, Secretary Feng, yes, how are you? How is your chief? Oh, yes, how I forget! Of course, he has gone to the old home to celebrate the birthday of his mother. My memory is so short these days! . . . Thank you for telling me . . . let me think it over, I'll ring you back . . . yes . . . yes . . . thank you."

He puts down the receiver, exhausted, and drops into an armchair like a bale of fine cotton. He closes his eyes a while and mumbles: "My memory is getting so bad. Only the other day I sent over the birthday screen for Commissioner Chang's mother and I seemed to have forgotten all about it just now. How awful!"

"What did Secretary Feng say?" Fang Wen-yu asks disconcertedly.

"He said the students are already out and asked me what to do." He smiles derisively. "Before we say anything to them, they are already trying to shift the burden on to us. If we had asked for protection, the whole bloody force of that Bureau would be operating from my house. The scoundrels! What is their duty?"

"But you say the students are already out!" Fang Wen-yu has no more idea of what to do than he, only his drug habit makes him more nervous. "What are you going to say to him?"

"Don't worry, he will telephone to his boss for instructions. I don't draw the salary of the Commissioner of Public Safety and I have no obligation to do his job for him." He looks at his desk calendar.

"But this place must have protection. We can't afford to take chances," Fang Wen-yu says.

"All right, Wen-yu, you ring up Chang Chi and ask him to send down fifty ruffians immediately, all armed, eighty cents per day for each person. They are far more reliable than the police."

Fang Wen-yu feels more settled. He immediately rings up Chang Chi. Pao Shan-chin also feels less worried and rests on the sofa with his eyes closed. Fang Wen-yu looks at him, not wanting to

think further about the matter, but what is he going to say to
the Secretary of the Bureau of Public Safety? He promised to
ring back, didn't he? The old chap is certainly calm! Pao Shan-
chin no longer remembers the presence of his guest. He knows
that if things get worse Fang will just quietly slink away; he
doesn't have to worry about him. He is counting over in his mind
the members of his family one by one. So long as they are all in,
there is not much to worry about. Suddenly he opens his eyes,
sits up and presses the bell, meanwhile calling, "Chen Sheng,
Chen Sheng!"

Chen Sheng runs in quickly and light-footedly.

"Is the eldest miss back yet?" He raises his head to look at the
calendar. "Isn't today Sunday?"

"Yes, this is Sunday, Master, and the eldest miss hasn't returned." Chen Sheng answers while he serves fresh tea.

"Telephone to the school and ask miss to come home at once.
Serve the tea later, telephone first."

Of all the daughters, he cares most for the eldest and is most
concerned over her conduct. She is *Taitai's* daughter, so he feels
more paternal towards her. There is even an element of respect
in his attitude. He of course loves the concubines' children, too,
perhaps even more, but the affection is a little different. Only in
his eldest daughter does he find something to identify the traditional virtues and morality of the family. She is *the* daughter. He
can't afford to let her do anything improper or anything that
exposes her to criticism. He has always wanted her to be a model
for the other women in the household. Her character must be
above reproach. If she should mix with her schoolmates in a public
demonstration, it would be a blow to his cherished hopes of her,
not to think of other consequences. And the idea of her coming
into frequent contact with boy students always presents premoni-
tions of the most dreadful kind.

"Master, the school telephone is cut!" Chen Sheng doesn't quite
want to put down the receiver.

"Send Little Wang to the school to escort her back. What's the

good of sticking that receiver to your ear all the time, you fool."
Pao Shan-chin's eyes bulge with anger.

Chen Sheng rushes out. Instantly there is the tooting of a motorcar horn. But no sooner has he disappeared than in he rushes
again, this time excitedly: "Master, Chang Chi is here with his
men!"

"Send him in." Pao Shan-chin's hands tremble slightly. The
name of Chang Chi has become associated with trouble, disaster,
and oftentimes bloodshed. With Chang Chi's presence he couldn't
help feeling that trouble is at his own door. A stroke of fear grips
him, though he knows that Chang Chi is here to protect him and
his family.

Chang Chi dares not advance beyond the threshold of the parlor. He stands outside, and says with a bow: "Your Excellency, I beg
your pardon, I've brought only thirty-five men, there is a shortage
of men because men are needed everywhere to handle the students.
I shall place these thirty-five men here first, and go and fetch
more. You needn't worry, Excellency. I'll make up the number
fifty before dark."

Pao Shan-chin glances at him patronizingly: "Very well. Are
they all armed? Good. Hurry up and get more men. Their pay
will be taken care of by the Commission. As to you, I'll personally
reward you."

"No, Your Excellency, don't reward me. Haven't I spent enough
of Your Excellency's money? If Your Excellency has no other
orders, I am going now." Chang Chi starts to go.

"No, wait a while. I've sent the car to fetch the eldest miss.
You wait until the car is back. Meanwhile, see to it that your
men are properly divided between the gate and the two entrances
to the *hutung*. Don't let them stay together in one place."

Chang Chi goes out to inspect his men. Pao Shan-chin turns
to Fang Wen-yu: "Wen-yu, what do you think? You don't think
it's going to be serious, do you?" He shuts the door and paces
up and down the room with his hands clasped behind his back.

"You never can tell." Fang Wen-yu also stands up, his face turning still paler. "The trouble is with the Bureau of Public Safety. Their boss not being here, that coward Feng is likely . . ."

"Is likely to run away," Pao Shan-chin finishes up for him. "A case of *The Empty City Strategem.*[4] Yes, there will be trouble, riot, and what not; anything can happen. We are in a jam, I can see. And yet we know nothing of the ringleader. What shall we do?"

The telephone rings again. Fang Wen-yu rushes to it without being told. "Who? Little Wang? Wait. Shan-lao, it's your man Little Wang, telephoning from somewhere up the street. He says that the students are already out in the streets. Your eldest daughter has joined the demonstration. The streets are in utter confusion. There has been already some hand-to-hand fighting."

"Tell Little Wang to come back immediately, Chen Sheng," he shouts out of the window, "tell Chang Chi to come in."

"Chang Chi, a reward of fifty dollars for you: you go and find the eldest miss for me, you know where her school is?"

"Yes, I do, but Your Excellency, how can I find her among the thousands of students in the streets? Even if I found her, I have no way of making her come home."

"You do your best. Try. If you find her, I'll give you an extra ten dollars."

"I'll go and try." Chang Chi appears none too optimistic.

"Little Wang is back, Master," Chen Sheng reports.

"Give me my hat, Chen Sheng." Pao Shan-chin seems hesitant for a moment, and turns to Fang Wen-yu. "Wen-yu, you stay here. I am going out to have a look at things. A young woman can't . . ."

"No, Shan-lao, no," Fang Wen-yu grabs his hand which is cold. "How can *you* go out, let me go. I am less known. Your photograph has just appeared in the papers! They will surely recognize you."

They simultaneously turn their eyes to the paper on the table.

[4] A famous Chinese play of the Three Kingdoms cycle. Surprised by the enemy, the hero made his lack of preparedness even more obvious than it really was by opening the city gates and revealing to the enemy his second-rate troops. Suspecting a trap, the enemy beat a hasty retreat.

"You can't go either, Wen-yu," Pao Shan-chin's legs begin to shake. He sits down. "How about asking Yamamoto what to do? This is not a small matter. It concerns my daughter. If he can send out a few of his private guards, they will find her, I am sure."

"Suppose he refuses to interfere, where will your face be?" Fang Wen-Yu says slowly in a suppressed voice.

"Listen to that!" Pao Shan-chin straightens up his back.

Chairman Pao's house stands near enough the street to hear the tooting of horns from passing automobiles. Now the sound is like the distant thunder of an approaching summer storm, a conglomeration of sounds not easy to analyze but definitely menacing and advancing like the furious tide in the Chientang.

Fang Wen-yu's face turns from paleness to a deathly green. He suddenly opens his mouth to swallow his breath as he begins to feel the need of drug. "Shan-lao, we have to get away!"

Pao Shan-chin's mouth twitches without uttering anything; his face turns scarlet. Torn between anger and fear, he becomes speechless. "The students! A group of idiotic brats!" He mumbles to himself, "What do you know? You want to put an end to my political career, eh? What harm have I done the people? What harm? You scoundrels!"

Chang Chi rushes in, forgetting to remove his hat. "Your Excellency, they are out, the students. I came up against them on my search for the eldest miss."

"Is the west entrance of the *hutung* well guarded?" Pao Shan-chin finally asks with some difficulty.

"They are not coming this way. They are going to gather at the parade grounds."

"If they come into the *hutung,* fire at them, I tell you," he seems less frightened when he hears that the students are not coming this way.

"Listen!" Chang Chi goes to the door and pushes it wide open.

"Down with the traitor!" Hundreds of voices shout simultaneously.

Pao Shan-chin's big eyes look round, as if to expect the words *mai kuo tsei* (traitor) to float down like a kite in the wind, but before he could see anything of the kind, there comes another wave of "Down with *mai kuo tsei*" in the air. He glances at Fang Wen-yu and Chang Chi and tries to force a smile but can't. He stutters out, "Chang Chi, where is the eldest miss? I told you to look for her, didn't I?"

"She is in this very group which is shouting the slogans now. There are lots of men in it too."

"Did you see her?"

"She is the one at the front carrying a big flag!"

"Down with the *mai kuo tsei!*" This time Pao Shan-chin seems to distinguish clearly the voice of his own daughter.

"Well, well!" his hands and lips continue to tremble. "A group of bandits and whores with 'no idea of the king and the father.' I'll get even with you yet! I can't control other people's daughters, but you, Miss Pao, you can't get out of my grip! Calling your father a traitor, eh? I'll fix you!"

"Shan-lao, Shan-lao!" Fang Wen-yu makes an effort to pacify him while trying to hold out against his opium-appetite; "Don't be angry, she is too young to know what she is doing. She can't be really against you. No. It can't be."

"You don't know." Pao Shan-chin trembles more nervously. "If she wants money or clothes, or a motorcar, she can tell me, she can have them all. Why should she choose to walk the streets shouting idiotic slogans? She is mad! Traitor, traitor! Your father a traitor! Do you like that? Fool! Shameless!"

The telephone rings, but no one cares to go to it. Fang Wen-yu pines away in the twilight stage of his opium-dream, while Pao Shan-chin seems too angry and crestfallen to make a move.

Presently Chang Chi walks over to the telephone. "Your Excellency, it's Secretary Feng of the Bureau of Public Safety," he said to Pao.

"Hang up, tell him I don't know what to do . . ." Pao Shan-chin lies down on the sofa.

"Chen Sheng, Chen Sheng!" Fang Wen-yu calls out faintly.

Chen Sheng comes in immediately from the courtyard.

Fang Wen-yu points to the direction of the inner court and thrusts out his lips making a faint purr like that of a cat.

Chen Sheng and Chang Chi retire together.

# The Letter from Home

## By Lao She (Lau Shaw)

It should have been an ideal family. There were only three of them, husband and wife and a three-year old son. But lack of numbers does not necessarily make for ideal conditions and this small family of theirs was not quite the miniature paradise that one might expect. On the contrary it was afflicted with its share of the bitterness of life.

From the uproar that came from the little family we might conclude that there was something abnormal about it and, furthermore, that it was about to go on the rocks as all things that deviate from the normal must.

For we could hear only the raised voice of the wife while the husband to all intents and purposes appeared to be a deaf mute. A more sympathetic interpretation of his silence would be, of course, that he hoped thus to maintain peace in the family. Unfortunately, his silence had a contrary effect on his wife.

"Why don't you say something?' she would scream. "Have you become dumb? Just for this I ought to divorce you, yes, divorce you!"

Yes, Fan Tsai-chu—the autocratic ruler of the family in question—was one of those modern women who know that there is such a thing in this world as divorce, though she did not know exactly what it means and involves. She did know, however, that it was a useful word which never failed to torture her husband. Her hair was done in the latest "aviation style" of 1937, she had a nice, soft complexion, her arms were round and firm, and her breasts were well developed and further accentuated by her tight-fitting clothes. When a woman like her threatens divorce, how can the husband fail to be frightened?

After one of these quarrels, she would give herself a careful appraisal in the mirror. She looked every bit like a motion picture star. She did not really dislike her husband—he was an attractive-looking man and very kind-hearted—but she felt constrained to nag him because it helped her to endure the injustice of her situation. He was not bad at all but "not bad" is not the same as "perfect." One of the things she had against him was that he earned only two hundred dollars a month. It was true that he turned over the entire amount to her and then received from her three or five dollars for his necessary expenses. But how could anyone reasonably expect two hundred dollars to do her justice?— play up to best advantage the beauty of her face, her arms, her breasts, her feet? Moreover, it was necessary for such a beautiful woman as she to keep up appearances. She did not mind buying a second-class ticket for the movies, because you sat mostly in the dark, but she would not tolerate any compromise when it came to the theater—it just had to be box seats. Under the circumstances how could one possibly manage on two hundred dollars? It was especially difficult to meet her own needs. Even by using on herself the money which should have been used for her husband and child, she could not afford pure silk stockings. Even by skimping on laundry she could not always hire an automobile for the theater trip but had to put up with those shabby rickshas that you hail from the street. Yes, old Fan wasn't bad at all. He never complained about food or anything else. But after all has been said and done, he still earned only two hundred dollars a month!

Fan loved his wife and child. He had made up his mind to marry a beautiful woman and to make this wish possible he had worked hard and lived frugally. He made sacrifices and denied himself all the little pleasures dear to young men of his age—cast them away like a prudent gardener so that he could cultivate his one Flower of Romance. He did not even smoke!

After he had saved enough money, he set out in search of his object in his new western-style suit made specifically for the purpose. He found Tsai-chu, pursued her, and married her.

She was not as beautiful as she fancied herself; she was not even as beautiful as the ideal that Fan had set for himself. But she was young and vivacious and she was well versed in the art of pretending to be what she was not. She succeeded in making Fan feel that if she was not his ideal she at least came close to it, that she would make a good appearance wherever she went. So he got out his savings and married her.

He was not burdened with those qualities which make for worldly success, but he was equipped with the kind of ability that made it possible for him to maintain his two-hundred-dollar income. He worked conscientiously so that he would not fall below the minimum standard which he had set for himself.

He soon found out what it was like to be married to a woman who mistakes superficiality for sophistication, hypocrisy for cleverness, cosmetics and clothes for beauty. But he did not regret it. He tried his best to please her, to show his love. He never answered her back. He did his utmost to gratify her whims. He wanted to be a model husband to her even if she did not quite turn out to be an ideal wife. Moreover, she was a mother, combining in her person the beauty of youth and of motherhood. He ought to be more considerate of her, yield to her whims and moods even more. After all, women are women. If one wants a woman, one just has to make allowances.

From his relations with Tsai-chu one can see what manner of man Fan was. He was extraordinarily faithful and conscientious. He never cared about rewards; he sought only to avoid mistakes. He put in three hundred dollars of effort for his two-hundred-dollar salary. He did this willingly without complaint. Because of this he was looked upon by his associates as a man without a future. Even when they imposed on him more than his share of the work, they called him a fool and were not grateful to him.

He did not belittle himself, however. As a matter of fact, he was quite proud of himself because he was sure that he was worth every cent that he got, because he could always get a job wherever he went. He never consulted the fortune tellers or bargained with the God of Luck. He sometimes compared himself to an ox and insisted that the ox had an honored place in the scheme of things.

Peiping and Tientsin fell as in a bad dream. Fan was then in Peiping. He must leave the city; his conscience would not allow him to accept a living from the enemy. But he could not leave because he had a wife who would not travel less than second class while he could only afford third class.

To Tsai-chu the world was only a huge amusement park whither she must go in her high heels, rain or shine.

"Where do you propose to go?" she demanded. "How could you be so cruel as to leave me and Hsiao-chu behind? Or do you expect me to tramp around like a refugee? If you'd only be sensible. What are you going to do with the furniture and things? Maybe you can travel around like a beggar but I can't. I can't get along without the little we have. Acting dumb again, eh? All right, if you can take along everything we have and travel with some degree of comfort I'll go with you. We have never had a chance to travel."

Fan said nothing. He did not want to criticize his wife's attitude. He did not want to desert his wife; but neither did he want to desert his country. He blamed the dilemma on himself, for if he had money he would be able to take his wife and child to free China.

For several days he did not go outside the house, not because he was afraid of personal danger but because he did not want to face the humiliation of bowing to the conquerors. He listened to his wife's complaints, played with Hsiao-chu, his eyes often blurred with tears.

"Hsiao-chu, you are a little *wang kuo nu*[1] now!" he said to his son one day when he felt particularly hopeless.

Tsai-chu heard him and said in an irritated tone, "What's the use of trying to sound noble? Take us to Hongkong if you don't like it here! What's the good of groaning if you can't do anything about it? Come here, Hsiao-chu. If only your papa were like Hsiao-chung's papa! They went to the concessions in Tientsin

[1] Literally "lost-country slave"; said of people who live under foreign rule.

with twenty trunks of clothes. And Hsiao-chung's mama is not as beautiful as I."

"Hsiao-chung's mama—her ears like this," Hsiao-chu said, pushing his ears forward with his plump little hands. He knew that this would please his mother; he had done it many times before.

One evening, after Tsai-chu and Hsiao-chu had gone to sleep, Fan slipped into the outer room. He put a piece of black cloth over the electric light and got out some letter paper. He would write her a note explaining why he must flee from the lost city, why it was better that he go alone first and send for her and Hsiao-chu after he had found a position. He made several starts but in the end gave up the attempt.

He tip-toed back into the bedroom and looked at his wife and child. In the dim light he could see only the outlines of their faces, but he knew those faces well, knew exactly where each mole and each scar was. Looking at them his heart softened and he lost the courage to leave them. It was stupid to perish together under the enemy's heels but it was human. He could not sleep at all that night.

But the call from outside the lost city persisted. It bade him get away quickly, rally under his own country's flag, and do his part in the country's salvation. If only Tsai-chu could understand, she would let him go. But he knew Tsai-chu; it would only cause a scene if he tried to explain his position to her.

Then a new idea occurred to him: he would present his case in a different light, explain that it was necessary for him to get away in order to improve their situation. That would be effective, that was the only thing Tsai-chu understood.

"As soon as I find a job I shall come for you and Hsiao-chu," he concluded. "I am sure you won't have to travel like a refugee."

"How about our immediate expenses?"

"I'll go and borrow some money. I'll leave it all to you."

"Where are you going to go?"

"Shanghai or Nanking, wherever the best opportunities for making money are."

"Don't forget to buy me some dress material in Shanghai!"

"I won't."

Thus Fan finally got away from Peiping and again saw the flag of free China. From Nanking he retreated with the government to Wuhan. He worked more industriously than ever. When he was not working he thought of his wife and child. He saved every penny he could and sent it to Tsai-chu. He wrote her regularly and at length of his work and apologized for the necessity of remaining away from her and Hsiao-chu. He looked for letters from her as he looked for reports of victories of the Chinese armies, but in vain. He knew that it was her way to remain silent except to demand more money, but he nevertheless worried about her and more especially about Hsiao-chu, for he also knew that Tsai-chu was not a very thoughtful mother.

In six or seven months he changed jobs no less than three times. It was not that he sought personal advancement but because he was getting to be known as a conscientious worker and was very much in demand. The war emergency had awakened in the government officials and others a new sense of responsibility and they were all eager to give the real workers a chance, though they themseles were not ready to put in their best efforts.

Finally a letter came while he was working in a military agency at Wuchang. He forgot everything else. He tore it open and read it with feverish excitement. He read it two or three times without actually comprehending what it said, so overwhelming were the images of his wife and child that the letter had conjured up. Yes, what about Hsiao-chu. He glanced through the letter again but found not a word about his son. Instead he found mostly words of complaint, cold unsympathetic words which chilled and benumbed him.

The air raid siren wailed. Automatically he started out for the shelter, still reading the letter and hoping to find words of reassurance of the safety of his wife and child. There were none. He read it yet another time, thinking, in his desperation, that perhaps the words were there but had somehow got misplaced and dissociated. But he found no fragments which he could piece together to spell such words as "safe" and "well." All he found was that she did not have enough money, that she could not afford any amusement or any new clothes. Why didn't he come back to them? He must be enjoying himself and have forgotten about his wife and child.

As the siren wailed its final warning Fan was still standing outside his building, still holding and staring at the letter. It was not until the enemy planes were almost directly overhead that he awoke from his trance. Then just as he started to run, a bomb fell almost directly on top of him. A large bomb fragment struck his head and almost cut it into two halves, spattering the letter with blood.

# A New Life

## By Chang T'ien-yi

When Mr. Li first came to the middle school looking for the principal, Mr. Pan, he created quite a stir among the faculty and the students. Was he then the well known writer and artist Li Yi-mo?

Both his heavy Chinese-style overcoat and the two heavy suitcases he was carrying were covered with dust. He was tall and thin and his complexion was dark. He must have gone without shaving for two weeks, for his chin was covered with an unsightly stubble of bristlelike hair. He was only about forty but looked like a man of fifty. Even his myopic spectacles were smeared with grime, like window panes which have not been washed for years.

If you had read his carefully embroidered essays, if you had seen the epithet of "leading exponent of pure art" which one of the reviews applied to him, you too would have been struck by the incongruity between his appearance and his reputation.

He spoke with great feeling to Principal Pan. "You may, Lao Pan, regard the old Yi-mo as dead. I have been dreaming the dream of the Southern Branch but I am now awake. I must thank the Japanese for this, for had it not been for the rude awakening which their guns brought about I would still be living the life of a hermit."

Li Yi-mo had fled with his wife and daughter when the enemy were about sixty or seventy li away. In normal times he was able to collect 700 piculs of rice in annual rent, but this year he had been able to collect nothing. He left his wife and daughter with his in-laws somewhere in the country in southern Chekiang, while he himself came here to look for his old friend Pan.

"I could not live under the shadow of the enemy's guns," he said. "I made up my mind to come to the rear and do my bit. I want to live a—a new life!"

Having learned that they needed a drawing teacher, he had come to volunteer for the job. That was to be his contribution during the national emergency.

"Imagine your condescending to teach in an obscure middle school like ours," Pan said half jokingly. "The honor is overwhelming . . ."

But Yi-mo stood up and said seriously, "Nonsense. I am a different man now. I used to emulate T'ao Yüan-ming [1] but now I want to be like Mo Ti. [2] I want to work and to suffer hardships as millions are doing. Moreover, it is no hardship at all to teach at a middle school; I am ready to teach in a primary school if necessary."

Thus Yi-mo began his new life. Besides teaching, he became one of the faculty advisers to the students cultural organization. He contributed articles to their weekly publication; he planned to make some drawings for propaganda purposes.

"We must publicize our cause to the entire world," he told his students. "We must tell everyone how just and peace-loving we are and how cruel and inhuman the enemy is. We are fighting not only for the existence of our country but for the honor and integrity of mankind."

He paced the class room nervously, his eyes fixed on the ground as if he was looking for something. Becoming conscious of the eyes fixed upon him, he glanced up at the students. He was so nervous and self-conscious that every time his eyes met another pair of eyes the clash was almost audible, like the impact of physical objects. He retreated to the window and looked out.

The weather was always bad here. The dark clouds always hung over you like a sheet of lead. The barren trees were dotted with crows, shivering and swaying in the cold wind. It was not

---

[1] Fourth-fifth-century poet who took little part in the life of his time.
[2] Ancient Chinese philospher who taught universal love.

yet five but the room was already dark. Outside the cold, gray light in the sky only accentuated the chilliness.

His thoughts turned to his own home. He used to stand before the window of his own studio when he was tired of working, and looked out at his garden, much as he was doing now. He recalled how cheerful his garden was, how green the moss was in his goldfish pond even in winter time. He wondered if his winter plum was in bloom now.

Then he stole a glance at his students, as if afraid that they were reading his thoughts. He must not moan for the comforts he had been accustomed to, he said to himself. During the cataclysmic times the nation was passing through, no one had the right to live in ease and comfort. He should be glad of the opportunities that his new surroundings gave him.

But in spite of his rationalizing he could not help heaving a long, inaudible sigh, for there was definitely something lacking in the new environment, though he could not say exactly what it was. He felt something oppressive over him which made it impossible for him to face the world with a joyous spirit. It vitiated the righteous indignation which had filled him and turned it into something sad and melancholy, and impotent.

From behind him came a sound which might have been a snicker or some one blowing his nose. He turned around slowly, looking somewhat sheepish, like a child who had to face a guest after he had been crying.

"What is your, er . . ." he said in an effort to cover up his embarrassment. "Do you draw things outside the class?"

The students grinned and looked at one another without answering.

"This is an elective course," Yi-mo said to them with an injured air. "Since you have elected it, I suppose I can assume that you are all interested in art. I hope you will all do as many propaganda drawings as you can and use them to arouse the people. All that is necessary is that they should be intelligible. It does not matter if they are artistically immature. This is no time to talk about art. We have no need of art as such during these times."

The students again looked at one another. After a while one with a closely cropped head made a pretense of standing up and said, "Mr. Li, how about these propaganda drawings? Do you call them art?"

"They are not," Mr. Li answered, with some degree of positiveness.

"Do you think, then, that no propaganda drawings can be considered art?"

These silly questions! How tiresome they are! However, Mr. Li explained his views patiently to them. Propaganda is propaganda; it is not and can never be art. He reiterated that the pressing need of the moment was for things which would awaken the people and keep up their morale. He began to gesticulate with his right hand as he warmed up to his subject.

"Our policy should be an eye for an eye and a tooth for a tooth.[3] If the enemy bombard us with guns, we must answer them with guns. The greatest of us are the soldiers at the front; the most useless are we so-called artists. We should abandon art for the time being and take up what every Chinese should be doing now . . ."

"Mr. Li," the student with the closely cropped head interrupted, making not even a pretense of standing up this time, "How about the works of Kaethe Kollwitz and the woodcuts of U.S.S.R.? They all serve propaganda purposes. Do you call these things art or not?"

"Another disciple of Lusin!" Mr. Li thought to himself. However, he tried to assume a tolerant air and thus temporized: "In the regard to this problem, er, er—this is not something which we can settle in a moment. It is a problem of aesthetics. It is very difficult to define just what makes art and what doesn't. Come to see me some time after class. I'll try to explain it to you."

But the student never came to see him, though he always turned in several drawings after their Wednesday afternoon class. Neither did any of the other students come to see him outside the class.

---

[3] This biblical expression has considerable currency among Chinese intellectuals; Lusin was among the first to urge its adoption by the oppressed.

It may have been because they were awed by his reputation and were reluctant to bother him, but then it was possible that they had no use for him. When a boy did come to see him on some business in connection with the school weekly, he always took his leave as soon as he was finished with the business in hand. Mr. Li was never sure when he passed by a group of students and heard some one say, "That's Li Yi-mo!" whether the tone was one of admiration or scorn.

They all seemed to like Mr. Chen, the physics and mathematics teacher. He was a short fellow, his face slightly pockmarked. He advised the students in many capacities and every Saturday evening he lectured at the People's Institute on war topics. He contributed to the school weekly on a variety of subjects, from characteristics of the dumdum bullet to the economic crisis of the enemy. He always nodded politely to Mr. Li when they met.

Lao Pan always spoke very highly of Chen. "He is the most public-spirited of us all," he would say. "He is so full of enthusiasm and so modest. He keeps up with the social sciences as well as with his own subject. You'll find him interesting to talk to."

"I am afraid that he works too hard," Li Yi-mo said with a faint smile. "His life must be a full one with nothing but work and work. I suppose you must like that kind of people; your life is much the same as his."

It was true, for Lao Pan had been principal of the school for nineteen years. Recently he had sent his family into the country and spent his nights as well as his days in the school. He had no other life than his job. The same was true of most of his colleagues.

One Saturday toward evening Mr. Li could endure it no longer. He walked into Pan's room like a somnambulist and said, "Lao Pan, the monotony of the life here is getting on my nerves. Let us go out and have something to drink."

"All right," Pan said. "But I can't drink. I have a heart condition."

"Doesn't anyone drink around here?"

"I am afraid not," Pan said shaking his head. "That is, no one but Mr. Chang, the one who teaches Chinese."

"How about getting him to go with us? What is he like?"

"What is he like?" Pan repeated, laughing. "Perhaps he can be best characterized by the stock phrase, "His conversation uninteresting, his face detestable.'"

Pan went on to tell his friend more about Mr. Chang in a more serious vein. Chang might be a learned man, he said, and he certainly was a good calligrapher. But he was not fit to teach Chinese in this day and age. He was opposed to the use of the vernacular and would not let his students write in that style.

"So you see what sort of person he is. Yet he has taught here for sixteen years. He can't be dismissed because he has a powerful connection. This is the educational system for you! Actually we are better off here than most places. What can you do unless you want to retire from the world entirely? If you want to do anything at all, you'll have to play along with such people and compromise."

Mr. Li yawned and lit a cigarette, giving Pan a look of commiseration.

"The man is reactionary to the core," Pan concluded. "When he gets on the subject of the war, his dialectic is simply that of a traitor."

That evening the two friends went to a restaurant and spent more than two hours there, with Li doing all the drinking and most of the talking. When Pan objected to the quantity of wine he was consuming, he put his hand on the pot and said, "Lao Pan, let me tell you what a devotee of the cup said. 'Hot wine is bad for the lungs, cold wine bad for the liver, but not drinking at all is bad for the heart. I would rather hurt my lungs and my liver than my heart.' This man really knew the secret of how to live . . . I pity you fellows who do not drink."

Thereupon he took another draught noisily and smacked his lips, throwing himself against the back of the chair in solid comfort.

"This wine is better than I expected. You must have a drink, just for a taste."

The other man complied then and said apologetically, "I used to have an occasional drink but I never could tell good wine from bad."

"This does not, of course, compare with what I have at home. I have nine crocks of old Shaohsing at home. It was said to be sixty years old. It may not be as old as that but it is safely thirty or forty years old. I used to invite friends of mine from the city to our little town to drink with me and talk. I don't really drink much; I only drink for the poetic mood that it creates. You have been to Hangchow, haven't you? Did you visit one of the wine shops there?"

"No."

"You ought to try them the next time you go there. The people you see there are the real devotees of wine. They can spend hours over a cup of old wine and a piece of mushroom-flavored dried bean curd."

He closed his eyes and recalled the beautiful porcelain cups that he used for wine. He remembered his box of seals, his books and pictures; he wondered what had happened to his eccentric fellow artists and collectors.

After this Mr. Li drank a little every day. He either went to the restaurant or sent out for it. He got more and more bored with life at school and asked himself why he had come here. He had written nothing and turned out but one drawing since he came. He passed his time copying the Drum Inscriptions, having borrowed a lithographic copy of it from Mr. Chang shortly after making the latter's acquaintance.

Mr. Chang was an oldish man with a florid face, slightly hunchbacked, and walking with a limp. He was not half as bad as Mr. Pan had made him out to be, Mr. Li thought. Moreover, he shared many of Mr. Li's hobbies. He liked to collect rubbings of inscriptions and seals. They became very friendly after they discovered their mutual admiration for the calligraphy of the Diamond Sutra engraved on the cliffs of Taishan.

"I have collected one thousand and five characters of this inscription," Li Yi-mo said proudly. "Even Yi Pei-chi hasn't that many. But now," he sighed, "I have no idea what has happened to my collection. Probably burned or carried off by the Japanese."

"That's why I have sort of lost interest in collecting such things," Mr. Chang chimed in quickly. "What's the use, in a time of strife like this. It is foreordained. Some people seem to like it; they would not rest until they had precipitated this war."

"But," Mr. Li objected mildly, "they attacked us first. If we did not resist . . ."

"Resist?" the other said with a sneer. "What are you going to resist with? What are you going to fight with? It only brings senseless suffering!"

"Then do you mean to say that we should let them come in and occupy our land?"

"I do not mean that, but, but—in a word, what's the use of bringing suffering upon yourself when it does no good?"

No wonder Lao Pan said that his dialectic is exactly that of the traitors, Mr. Li said to himself.

The older man continued, wiping a speck of foam from the corner of his mouth: "For instance, the Japanese generally behave pretty well when they first occupy a place. But then come the guerrillas and subversive elements. Naturally the Japs will carry out raids and arrests and otherwise make the lot of the common people unbearable . . . What good are the guerrillas? They can't really put up a fight. They can only make surprise attacks. When enemy reinforcements come, they flee, leaving the innocent to suffer . . ."

"But reports indicate that the common people welcome the guerrillas," Mr. Li protested, amused at himself for raising such useless objections. "In many places the guerrillas are simply organized for self-defense, by the common people, unwilling to stand by and watch their land ravaged by the enemy."

"Self defense? *Heng,* do you have any artillery? Do you have any guns to match the enemy's? It only brings more confusion, more suffering."

"Do you mean to say, then, that we should live under them as willing subjects? traitors to our own country?" Mr. Li had a mind to retort, but did not. He suddenly recalled an article he had read in the school weekly, entitled "On Traitors of a Certain Type." It might well have been written with Mr. Chang specifically in mind. He did not realize how cogent the article was until he now heard exactly the same kind of argument from Mr. Chang.

He lit a cigarette and puffed at it vehemently. He felt flushed in the face and his hand shook. He wanted to stand up and denounce this fellow Chang and explain to him the necessity of adopting guerrilla tactics, how they had turned the enemy's rear into front lines, how they had prevented the enemy from making full use of the large cities that they captured at great sacrifice. But he did nothing of the kind. He was not accustomed to discourse on such topics. Moreover, what he had in mind to say had been said before; he did not want people to say that Li Yi-mo was given to mouthing the sentiments of others. He recalled that he had read somewhere that the first man who compares a woman to a flower is a genius but that the second man who does so is an imbecile.

He contented himself with asking Mr. Chang if he had been reading the weekly. The latter retorted that he did not understand stuff written in the vernacular.

For a long while both were silent. Li Yi-mo wished he could break away gracefully, or that some one else would drop in and relieve the embarrassing situation. He noticed that the other man was looking at his cigarette, so he offered him one. Chang lit it and inhaled deeply. He also held it away at his arm's length so as to read its brand. Then feeling obligated to say something after accepting the smoke, he asked Li how many cigarettes he smoked a day.

"I hear that you like a little wine occasionally," Chang said, in a further attempt to make conversation.

"Yes," Li answered. "But I have not been able to find any one to drink with." He looked at Chang expectantly.

"In that case you must come to my house for a drink soon."

Li suggested that they go to the restaurant that same evening and Chang accepted the invitation after protesting politely that he should have the pleasure of playing host first.

After this the two men were often seen together, much to the surprise of Pan, the principal.

"Do you find much in common to talk about?" Pan asked his friend one day.

"That doesn't matter much," Li answered, somewhat displeased at the question, which to him seemed like an attempt to interfere with his life. "Friends do not have to share the same views on everything. In fact it enriches one's life to have all types of friends. As for Mr. Chang and myself—we have a lot in common so long as we do not talk about current events. Such as poetry, painting, and calligraphy . . ."

But actually Mr. Li was beginning to find Chang's company irksome. The latter was always boasting about his collection of paintings and such things, but he never showed any of it, on the few occasions that Li visited him at his house. He was always threatening to play host but never did. The best he could do was to regale Li with slanderous gossip about members of the faculty and some of the more prominent students.

Li began to shun his drinking companion and took to drinking by himself. He loathed his surroundings more and more. He wished the war would end soon so that he could return to his own home and its comforts. He recalled Irving's story of Rip Van Winkle and wished that he could wake up one morning and find China prosperous and at peace, after years of desperate struggle.

No, he must not allow himself to take such a passive attitude. He must rouse himself and take an active part in the struggle and hasten China's emancipation. But he could not think of anything better than Aladdin's lamp or the three wishes that the gods sometimes grant in fairy tales. He proceeded to think of the three wishes that he would make, three positive and constructive wishes . . .

The next morning he did not wake up until ten. He felt a bitter taste in the mouth and was annoyed at himself for having indulged in childish, wishful thinking which only kept him awake. He stretched and walked over to his desk and tore off a sheet from the calendar.

"Another Sunday!" He muttered with a sigh.

That indefatigable fellow Chen had apparently gone out already, for he left a note asking him to attend the editorial conference of the school weekly at one o'clock.

"These meetings and conferences!" he muttered again, throwing aside the note.

The room was flooded with sunlight. The birds chirruped in the garden as if trying to drown out the singing and shouting students. What was there to sing and shout about, Mr. Li asked himself with a frown.

He read the paper while he sipped his pot of Kimon, a tea of a quality far below what he was accustomed to. He wondered how the *laopaihsing*—the common people—in the occupied territories lived. They probably carried on business and cultivated the land much as before. If he had not fled his home, he could probably collect his rents as before and paint pictures and carve seals as he used to. These things had nothing to do with politics and the war. As long as he did not write anything against the Japanese, they would probably leave him alone.

The accounts of enemy atrocities reminded him of other accounts he had read. He sighed regretfully.

Only in Peiping it was different. It fell peacefully to the enemy and as a consequence had been able to live in peace. Was it not true that some of the intellectuals had gone back there, after braving the unaccustomed rigors of the interior in war time?

He found himself ranting against the guerrillas much as Mr. Chang had done. It was they who forced the enemy to adopt retaliatory measures.

"Traitor! Traitor!" He clenched his hand as he suddenly realized where he had heard these familiar sentiments. "We must eradicate such elements in our midst. I'll bring the matter up at the conference and urge a vigorous campaign against traitors like him . . ."

For a moment he even considered writing a piece against Mr. Chang then and there but upon further reflection he decided that he was perhaps not in the best position to criticize.

He must not be so objective and analytical. That was bound to make one feel sad and unhappy. Perhaps he was not being fair to himself. Perhaps the real reason why he did not take up the pen was because he was not in the mood.

To escape from himself, he decided to drop in on Pan. He must try to divert himself from his own thoughts. Introspection would only make things worse.

But unfortunately Pan had a caller, with whom he appeared to be in earnest conversation. "I have no place here," he thought to himself. "They are apparently engaged in an important conversation, probably trying to settle the problems of this world once for all. You couldn't very well interrupt them and ask Lao Pan to keep you company while you drank, could you?"

He gestured to Pan not to disturb himself and beat a hasty retreat. He walked out of the school gate and unconsciously bent his steps in the direction of his drinking companion's house. He encountered groups of students returning to the school for dinner but he paid no attention to them.

"I should hope that one could have at least one day's freedom out of the week," he said to himself vindictively. "I refuse to go to the conference just for spite. Who is this fellow Chen to order me around? I don't care if they do criticize me. Everyone must be allowed to live his life in his own way. *Heng!* could it be a crime, then, to look up old Mr. Chang and take him out for a drink?"

Having thus justified himself, Mr. Li redoubled his steps in the direction of Mr. Chang's house.

# House Hunting

## By Tuan-mu Kung-liang

Almost everyone who has to retreat from Wuhan and make his way to Chungking gets a headache the minute he considers the housing problem. Everyone knows there isn't any room for another rat, of which there is a superabundance in the nation's provisional capital.

This was the situation which Miss Huang Kuei-chiu had to face and she did not like it at all. The hotels are too expensive and they are, besides, very noisy. According to *At Your Service,* the sheet published by the Min Sheng Steamship Company and distributed free to the passengers, even the old-fashioned inns with

> Find lodgings for the night before it gets dark
> Rise for the journey before the cock crows

pasted on their gates were full. When she remarked to the steward on the crowded condition of the boat, the latter answered sympathetically but at the same time ominously, "It *is* terrible, hsiaochich, but it is even worse in Chungking."

She'd certainly be squeezed in like a sardine in the can, Miss Huang said to herself. She saw before her an ocean of people, with bobbing heads and swirling feet, muddier and more turbulent than the waters of the Yangtze. She would probably have to sleep on the street when she got to Chungking.

The electric fan directed a stream of humid, warm air at her; outside there was a steady buzz of voices. She felt faint and decided to go out on deck. She rose from her upper berth and noticed, as she put on her shoes, the man in the opposite berth appraising her legs. "Bother!" she thought to herself as she hurried out. The deck was crowded with passengers chattering and gesticulating toward shore. She found the smell of sweat unbearable and scuttled like a tortured fish into the dining room. Two men were talking.

"That's the way things are now."

" 'The road to Shu is hard, harder than mounting to the sky.' It is not so hard to get there now; the problem is to find a place to stay."

The conversation irritated her; she did not have to be reminded of her troubles. What a bother! Why had she ever thought of going to Szechwan?

Suddenly a way out occurred to her. She'd have a place to stay, absolutely. Why didn't she think of Commissioner Li before? Surely he would have a room to spare. He was a former schoolmate of hers and moreover . . . Even if he did not have a spare room, he'd have to spare one anway. The more she thought about it the more sure she became. She felt immensely relieved. The problem was solved. She would have a nice, comfortable place to stay, better than she had dared to hope. She went back to her cabin in high spirits.

Yes, Commissioner Li was her schoolmate. In the old days they all called him "Big Horn." He had pursued her and had once proposed to her on bended knees. There was no question of his refusal. He should consider it a favor, congratulate himself that the emergency of the time had thrown this good fortune into his lap.

She counted her money and felt reassured now that she did not have to worry about rent.

Miss Huang had been a music teacher at the Women's Normal School at Hankow. When the school closed because of the tense situation, her sister in Canton had suggested that she go there. Cost of living there was low, her sister wrote, and the same clothes would do the year around. Her sister also spoke highly of the Cantonese character. She described them as a courageous and enterprising people, and easy to get along with, and said that if worst came to worst they could flee to the South Seas. However, she did not go to Canton because it was then subjected to heavy air raids.

Now she was glad that she was going to Szechwan. She recalled the famous lines—

Of the three gorges of Patung, the Wu Chieh is the longest,
Where the moaning monkeys bring tears to the traveler's eyes.

and other tributes paid to the land of Shu. She planned to sail on the Chialing, famed for its clear, blue waters, and to climb Mount Omei, to which pilgrims flock from all over China. It would be nice to find a regular job, but she could always take up patriotic work. With everything thus solved, Miss Huang went to bed and slept soundly that night.

Arriving at Chungking she left her things with a former colleague and after tidying up herself, she put on her best dress and set out for Commissioner Li's house. She had his address already but she went to the Tax Commission to make sure. She was pleased to learn that he did have a large house.

How was she to broach the subject? Why, she need not beat about the bush. She'll make a frontal attack.

"Commissioner Li . . ."

She smiled at the incongruity. It is better to address him as she used to in school, Mister Li or even "Big Horn." However, she decided to address him as Commissioner Li.

"Commissioner Li. I have just arrived in Chungking and can't find any vacancy at the hotels. You'll just have to get a room for me. I must have it right away." If he should hesitate, she'd say, "Why can't you let me have one of your spare rooms? I am sure you have lots of room." She again recalled the proposal scene when he knelt awkwardly before her and calling, "Kuei-chiu! Kuei-chiu!" She could not help feeling a warm spot in her heart for him.

Chungking looked quite impressive with the Szechwan Salt and the Mei Feng towers dominating the scene. There was quite an array of neon signs, which gave the city an air of prosperity. Chungking was much better than she had expected. It was in fact an imposing metropolis.

Suddenly a group of students in boy-scout uniforms surrounded her ricksha asking for contributions. "Bother!" she again said to herself. She had just arrived and was asked to contribute before she had a chance to eat or find a place to live."

"I have contributed."

"Please contribute some more."

"I have really contributed. I have just come from Hankow."

"Please!" one pleaded with a salute.

They could not make her contribute, salute or no salute. She told the ricksha man to go on. The disappointed youngster stared after her. She was so well dressed but would not give anything. On her side Miss Huang felt that they had no business to annoy her when she had so much trouble of her own. She cursed the stupidity, the lack of common sense on the part of those conducting the drive. How could they expect people to contribute money when they were not feeling right?

Not far ahead she was stopped by another group of scouts, even more persistent than the group she had just fled. One of them even asked if she did not want to be patriotic. But Miss Huang would not give in, though she was flushed with embarrassment. She turned up her nose and ordered the ricksha man to go on.

What persistent pests! She had never seen the like of them. They had spoiled the day for her. She wished again that she had never come to Szechwan.

Well, Szechwan is not such a bad place after all. She would be able to feast on *yin erh* from Tungkiang, candied peaches from Hochow, orange liqueur from Luchow, and to get celebrated Chengtu furniture. The last reminded her of what her former colleague had told her of the bamboo furniture of Chungking.

"It is excellent," she had said. "It is cheap and elegant. It will appeal to your artistic taste. Even Chairman Lin Sen furnishes his house with it. It is so simple and durable."

She would refurnish her room. "Big Horn's taste leaves something to be desired. It would look well too if she brought her own furniture. She'd say, "I have ordered the furniture. You can send some one for it."

So she told the ricksha man to take her to a furniture shop. There she picked out a whole set of things made of rattan and bamboo. She especially liked the bed. And it all cost only thirty-five dollars, including a sweetmeat tray and tea table. It was a lot of money considering the state of Miss Huang's finances, but that couldn't be helped since she wanted to impress Commissioner Li. She would be saving rent any way. So she concluded the deal by paying a five-dollar deposit.

She was very pleased with herself, so she gave the ricksha man a thirty-cent tip. She turned to look for the doorbell but, not finding it, she used the knocker. Soon after she was ushered by a servant into the parlor a young woman came in, without question the lady of the house.

This was something Miss Huang had not thought of and she had not the slightest notion of what to say to her. She had not foreseen that she would run into Mrs. Li first.

"Whom do I have the pleasure . . ." Mrs. Li began, but then recognized her. "But of course, I remember now. You are—Miss Huang. You are very kind to come to see us. I suppose you have been in Chungking for some time."

"Not so very long," Miss Huang answered. "I wanted to come to see you people as soon as I could." It's all over! She was not prepared for Mrs Li.

The Commissioner himself now ambled in.

"Chung-ching," Mrs. Li called to him. "It is so kind of Miss Huang to come to see us." Then turning to Miss Huang, she said, "I don't suppose you come out much. Where do you live? I want to come and see you tomorrow."

"Don't you bother," Miss Huang temporized. "I am staying with a relative."

"On what street? I know Chungking well. Let me come and see you."

"It is in some side street, very inconvenient. It is so hard to find anything."

"Isn't that so though . . ."

Commissioner Li broke in, "You ladies visit for a while. I must get ready to go to the office." He looked at his wrist watch as he went upstairs. "You must have dinner with us, Miss Huang. I won't stay long at the office."

"How do you like our furniture? Chung-ching got everything from Chengtu. It's very cheap. The camphorwood table cost only ten dollars. In Shanghai it would cost at least sixty.

"Chung-ching has been very busy since the war. As you know our national revenue is derived from three principal sources, customs, salt, and direct taxes. Now, with the first two sources largely in enemy hands, direct taxes are playing a more and more important part. It is very hard on Chung-ching.

"Recently he has been even busier than usual. He has taken on a drive for winter clothes for the soldiers at the front, you see. It is something which we who enjoy the comparative security and comfort of the rear cannot shirk. Our consciences would not allow it. So Chung-ching took an active part in organizing the drive and that keeps him very busy on top of his other duties. I have always said that as long as the bombs have not fallen on our heads, we should, unless we are entirely cold-blooded, do our part for the country—let everyone do what he can, let those who have money contribute money and those who have brawn contribute brawn. Chung-ching . . ."

Commissioner Li came down stairs. He had changed into a gown of satin with round medallions on it. Over it he wore a short black jacket.

"I am very glad that you came, Miss Huang," he said with an ingratiating smile. He walked up to Miss Huang and pulled up a tea table before her. On the table was a brass ink box, a brush, and seal ink. "You must be generous, Miss Huang. 'The more you contribute the more blessed you will be; the less you contribute the more cursed you will be.'" What a vulgar fellow Big Horn was, trying to solicit money by high pressure.

"Here is Mrs. Yeh. You know her, class of 1935, maiden name Wu Lu-shih. One hundred dollars. The second contributor used to be on one of the college teams. He is at present working at the Farm Bureau. I think he was an assistant in the department of economics for a while. His contribution is too small, only twenty dollars. Look here at Professor Su's pledge, two hundred dollars. He occupies first honor so far. Kuei-chiu, you must do your share to help our brave warriors at the front. Winter sets in earlier up around Hankow. The need is urgent . . . Do you mind if I smoke?"

"Not at all," Miss Huang said. "How much should I contribute?" she said modestly, giggling a little. "What day of the month is it today?" she asked, glancing around for a calendar.

Her host reached for the calendar on the desk, glanced at it and said, "It is the eighth."

"It is my custom," Miss Huang said, smiling bewitchingly at Commissioner Li, "to contribute the same amount as the date on the calendar."

"Maybe I should ask you at the end of the month."

"If you don't like it, maybe I won't contribute anything after all."

"All right, all right," Commissioner Li said, drawing the book toward him and taking up the brush.

Miss Huang took a ten dollar bill and gave it to her host. The latter said, imitating the local merchants, "I have no change." That Big Horn was always trying to be funny.

Then he took up the brush and wrote in the book: "Miss Huang Kuei-chiu, $10. Solicited by Li Chung-ching."

Miss Huang herself stared vacantly at the camphorwood furniture brought from Chengtu.

# Under the Moonlight

## By Kuo Mo-jo

The child had been buried in the earth, and it was some time since the two workmen who had helped Yi-ou went away with their spades. The sky was dark except for a growing patch of light on the eastern horizon, herald of the rising moon. There wasn't a breath of air or the slightest sound anywhere. The trees around him and the grains in the field had survived the parching heat but had not yet recovered strength enough to breathe freely.

Yi-ou had always thought that he would die before his children. How ironical that he whose body was wasted by tuberculosis should have managed to survive more than a year of wartime hardship while a new sprout should pine away after a brief illness of only five days!

Sitting there on the grass before the little mound of earth, his head buried in his hands, Yi-ou looked like a sepulchral lion, grotesque because he was disproportionately large as compared to the mound.

The moon emerged from behind the cloud. It was almost full. But across the sky on the other side a dark cloud bank was forming and there were flashes of lightning darting through it.

Tentatively the insects commenced their night song.

A few uneven rays of light sifted through the bamboos and shone upon the head of the lion-shaped man.

Slowly Yi-ou raised his head and looked at the moonlight from under his cream-colored sun helmet. His sunken eyes were red and his cheek bones were sharply defined. His face was pale and his lips twitched from time to time.

He fumbled around him until he found his bamboo cane and

struggled to his feet. He was somewhat under medium height. He wore a cotton suit of the same color as his helmet and both showed evidences of having seen five years of war and having accompanied their owner through all his wanderings until he came to this village not far from the provisional capital.

He turned his back to the moon and stood facing the little mound.

"Sleep well, I-erh," he said aloud. "You will be more comfortable here than sleeping by the side of your consumptive papa or by the side of your worn-out mama. There will be no mosquitoes to bother you here, no sickness or hunger or cold to plague you. Sleep well, my child . . .

"I-erh, your papa wouldn't be able to take care of you for very long any way. He has only neglected you. Your mama has been worn out. Since the war she has borne you three one after another. We have fled from Nanking to Wuhan and from Wuhan to Chungking. During these years she has had to take care of everything. Now she has to take care of your sick papa too. I know you do love your mama. Sleep well then. You won't need your mama to fan you to sleep now."

He felt a suggestion of tears but nothing came just as nothing came of the sky which had promised rain but had only given a display of lightning. The clouds which had risen vigorously like thick smoke dissipated just as quickly. The moon sang a triumphant song.

The thin, emaciated man moved slowly along the edge of rice fields, dragging his long, heavy shadow after him like an underfed horse dragging a field gun up a hill. His bamboo cane echoed the encouragement of the frogs: "Quite right, quite right, we must help the man to the end."

From the rice fields he dragged his shadow to a river, where he followed the bank, and then across a long stone bridge. He cut across another rice field and turned into a farmyard facing the east. Here the shadow fell in front of him. It was as if he had at last tired of dragging it and decided to push it from behind. Finally he came to a building to the right of the yard, where in the shadow of the house he was able to shake off his burden at last.

This was Yi-ou's home.

He took off his helmet and wiped his forehead with his sleeves. For a while he stood there panting.

There was no light inside, but as soon as he stepped over the doorsill he could hear a weak moaning from the inner room to the right. He hurried over in that direction. It was even darker in there and he could make out almost nothing. Just inside the door a bamboo couch lay across his path inviting a collision, but he managed to skirt it.

The sound of moaning came from a large bed at the far end of the room. As he made his way through the crowded room, his eyes gradually became accustomed to the darkness and he was able to make out the scene before him. His wife was sitting on a small bamboo chair and was leaning over the bed and scratching the back of their daughter. At the other end of the bed slept their youngest child, who had also been sick. Leaning his cane against the bed, he put his hand over the child's forehead. It was still feverish. As the child wore only a light vest, he pulled a piece of cloth over its belly.

"He will only pull it off," the mother said in a sad, resigned voice. It was as she said. The child reached down and pulled away the cloth.

"I suppose you haven't had your dinner yet," he asked, after standing there helplessly for a while.

"I can't swallow a thing," she said. "A little while ago Chen-erh pestered me to take her to see I-erh, but I was able to get her mind off it by giving her a piece of cake."

She had been with I-erh at the hospital until the latter's death. It was not until that afternoon that Yi-ou went to relieve her and take care of the burial.

There was a suffocating smell of mosquito incense.

"You might as well go to bed yourself," he said to his wife. "The smoke will only annoy Tsun-erh." He took a box of matches hanging from the curtain hook and lit a vegetable oil lamp on the desk.

Silently his wife crawled up into the bed, fanned out the mosquitoes and let down the curtain flaps.

Yi-ou hung his cane and helmet on the clothes tree. He also took off his coat and hung it up. Then he stamped out the mosquito incense under the bed.

The desk was littered with books and papers, medicine and soy milk bottles. A bundle of mail attracted his attention. It was sent to him every morning from the office where he worked. Ordinarily he looked forward eagerly to the Chungking papers, which he did not get until late in the afternoon. He was most concerned with the war news from Europe; next came the news of literary activities. On this occasion, however, he put the newspaper aside and took up two letters first. One was quite heavy. He opened it and pulled out a bundle of banknotes wrapped around with a sheet of letter paper on which was written the following:

I-ou: I am enclosing a thousand dollars which the Writers' Fund Committee sent today. It is a grant for your medical expenses. Please accept this and send them a receipt. I hope you will be reasonable in this matter. You must know that all your friends are very much concerned over your health and that the Committee has given you this grant out of a deep appreciation of your work. The acceptance of this will not hurt your reputation in the least, so please do not be stubborn. I wish you all the best. Have the little ones got over their illness?

TUNG-FENG.   *July 7*

The grant came to him as no surprise. For some time his friends had been thinking of getting him a grant from the Committee but had hesitated because they knew his scruples. Recently when they heard that his children were sick they decided to apply for it anyway.

Yi-ou felt bound to heed the advice of Tung-feng, a respected friend and the chief of his division. They had held his position open for him though he had been sick for more than a year. His duties had been taken over by his friends. Because of these things he was more than usually loyal to his organization and grateful to Tung-feng. However, he was still undecided. He pushed aside the letter and the notes and took up the other letter.

This was from the library of one of the universities, from which he had borrowed six books more than two years ago. Unfortunately these had been destroyed with his own books when the place where he worked was bombed. But the letter aroused in him a sense of obligation that he could not ignore. "We earnestly hope that you will return these books as soon as possible," the letter read; "for they cannot be replaced now and are urgently needed for reference purposes." What was he to do? How was he to return them now if they could not be bought on the market? He turned his eyes to look at the bundle of notes.

Threre was another fit of groaning, and as he turned in that direction he was shocked to see by the shadow cast on the mosquito curtain how thin he had become.

A desperate thought flashed across his mind as his eyes rested on a coil of rope slung over the head of the bed. It was used for tying baggage and was not very thick. He went over and felt it in his hand. Then he lifted the flap of the curtain and looked inside. His wife was sitting up, rubbing the younger child's belly and shedding tears as before.

He let down the curtain flap and retreated. He lay down on the couch and began to figure out how to make use of the thousand dollars.

The money had come at a very opportune time indeed. He would have to accept it.

The six books he had lost were not rare. Before the war they would have cost about ten dollars at most, but now they must cost two or three hundred. Yes, he should pay for the books that had been destroyed, he must send three hundred dollars to the library.

Books are valuable things. He himself had misled some of his young friends because he did not make full use of them.

> They gathered lotus seeds in Kiangnan,
> And how the lotus leaves did grow *tian tian*.

Two years before he had misinterpreted the meaning of the last two characters when he gave a talk before the Juvenile Players.

Later, in thumbing through the *Tz'u Yuan* he had unexpectedly come across the expression. It was not until then that he realized thas the characters constituted an onomatopoetic expression describing the profuseness of the lotus leaves. He must redeem his mistake by presenting the group with a set of the *Tz'u Yuan*. That would mean another two hundred dollars, the market price of the small print edition.

Before I-erh died an arrangement had been made for him to enter the nursery school. Though I-erh was dead, he was none the less grateful to the school for consenting to take him. If the boy had not died, it would have been necessary to buy some clothes and things for him and that would have come to at least five hundred dollars. He would act just as if I-erh had not died and contribute the sum to the school.

That still left to be taken care of the four hundred dollars he had borrowed from his landlord for the burial of I-erh.

He would have to ask Tung-feng to help him—to take care of the disposition of the thousand dollars and to pay this other debt for him. There was nothing else to do.

He struggled up to his feet and went over to the desk. He found a sheet of manuscript paper and took out the only brush that had a brass cap on it to keep it moist. He dipped the brush in the ink box and began to write in a fine, regular hand:

TUNG-FENG HSIEN-SHENG:

I am very grateful to you. I am accepting the thousand dollars as you have suggested, but there are a few requests that I have to make of you.

1. A year ago I borrowed six books from the library of the —— University. Unfortunately these were destroyed in an air raid while we were living in the city. Now the library is dunning me for these books (I am enclosing their letter) but I have no way of replacing them. Please send them three hundred dollars out of the thousand as reimbursement for the loss of the books.

2. Before my illness I gave a series of lectures before the Juvenile Players. In one of the lectures I misinterpreted the expression *tian tian* in the lines

> They gathered lotus seeds in Kiangnan,
> And how the lotus leaves did grow *tian tian!*

This has been on my mind ever since. So I want you to send two hundred dollars to the Players for them to buy a set of the *Tz'u Yuan*.

3. I-erh died this morning and will not, therefore, be able to take advantage of the arrangement you made for him to enter the nursery school. However, I want to act as if I-erh had not died, and so beg you to send five hundred dollars to the nursery as a token of my appreciation of their kindness.

4. I had to borrow four hundred dollars from my landlord in order to bury I-erh. Since I am penniless at the moment, I beg you to pay this debt for me.

I am sure that you will forgive me for imposing these things on you as I am sure that you will grant them. I wish you health and happiness forever.

I-ou. *Midnight, July 27*

After finishing the letter he put it in a large envelope, together with the money and other things he had for the office and wrote on the outside Tung-feng's name.

The desperate thought kept flashing through his mind. Though he did not say a word about it in the letter, what was implied was as clear as the shadow which the lamp cast on the mosquito curtain.

He was not only thinking of exploring the unknown himself but was thinking of taking with him his wife and his remaining children.

"You had better go to bed, Chen-erh's father," his wife called to him. "What are we going to do if you suffer a relapse?"

He felt like crying again, but his eyes were dry as before.

He put the letter in his trousers pocket, blew out the lamp, and went to the couch and lay down.

He had intended to wait, to wait until his wife fell asleep, but his tired body asserted its needs.

The moon shone into the room through a skylight window. It struck the clothes tree and then began to crawl forward like a thing alive.

For a long, long time Yi-ou did not stir at all, nor did he wake up when his wife got off the bed and gently let down the round mosquito net over him.

The insects chirruped on incessantly all around.

*July 29, 1942*